THE GIRL AND THE SECRET PASSAGE

A.J. RIVERS

The Girl and the Secret Passage
Copyright © 2023 by A.J. Rivers

All rights reserved. Without limiting the rights under copyright reserved above, no part of this publication may be reproduced, stored in or introduced into retrieval system, or transmitted, in any form, or by any means (electronic, mechanical, photocopying, recording, or otherwise) without the prior written permission of both the copyright owner and the above publisher of this book.

This is a work of fiction. Names, characters, places, brands, media, and incidents are either the products of the author's imagination or are used fictitiously. The author acknowledges the trademarked status and trademark owners of various products referenced in this work of fiction, which have been used without permission. The publication/use of these trademarks is not authorized, associated with, or sponsored by the trademark owners.

PROLOGUE

Why is no one helping?

HER FEET POUNDED HEAVILY INTO THE SIDEWALK, THE SOUND LIKE a steady heartbeat thudding around her in the cold air. Her breath billowed in white clouds around her face, and she inhaled it as stinging ice crystals until her throat felt raw. But she still screamed. She still forced past the sharp pain and the taste of blood to cry out to anyone who could be listening.

Why aren't they listening?

She could hear them. She knew the city was alive, the streets awake, the light pouring from windows and doors carrying voices, laughter, shouting, breath. They were there. She didn't know who they were. She couldn't call out their names. But they were there. None were listening.

Streetlights meant to offer guidance and comfort felt like they were betraying her. Their hazy pools of glow freezing in the December night air dissolved away the shadows that offered her protection on the sidewalk. She knew this area. She knew the turns in the cracked concrete of the sidewalk and the narrow alleys like veins through the buildings. She'd pretended to hide in them before. Her feet had danced across the concrete then. The clicking of her shoes had snapped and the sound of her laughter had floated in the air. She knew the feeling of the building wall against her back, the rough surface of the brick sticking to her skin as she melted into it with summer heat and the kisses she was really hiding.

She was still shouting as she ran into one of them, but the pain in her throat kept the sound down. It was barely above the sound of her feet and the gasp of her frozen breath. They were so loud she didn't know if she could actually hear them behind her. The sound of their boots might have been the pounding of her heart against her ribs. She wouldn't look back to find out.

She ran down the alley and ducked down at the side of a dented blue dumpster streaked with rust and remnants of what had been tossed inside. Curled back against it, she tried to hold her breath to stop any sound or the white puffs of air from revealing her. Even as she crouched there, she knew she'd made a mistake.

This was every horror movie she had ever watched with her friends. It was every TV show about a serial killer. It was every moment she laughed at the stupidity of the girl on the screen and shouted at her not to make herself such an easy target. Don't run upstairs. Don't go down in the basement. Don't look back over your shoulder.

She had nowhere to go.

But she had to try.

Launching herself from the corner beside the dumpster, she ran to the end of the alley and jumped up onto the chain-link fence at the end. The throb of music vibrated slightly through the metal. She hated the feeling of those vibrations against the palms of her hands. They blocked her voice. They made it sound like her cries for help were just the rhythm of another night in the music-fueled district of the city.

She scrambled up the fence as fast as she could force her cold, tired legs to move. The rubber soles on her shoes were thick, making them harder to fit into the holes of the fence so she could push herself upward. One got caught, and she let out a desperate sob as she tried to pull it out. She knew they were behind her now. There was no pretending their breath was wind or their oppressive presence was just the energy of the countless people crammed into dim buildings and anonymous corners.

THE GIRL AND THE SECRET PASSAGE

She grabbed the top of the fence and cried out as a barbed wire hidden among years of kudzu overgrowth bit through her gloves and into her hands. The metal tangled with the yarn stitches designed to keep her warm. It held her in place until they clamped onto her by her hips and wrenched her down onto the cold pavement. The crack of her head on the ground sounded like something being tossed into the dumpster. She was aware of it from a distance. Like the pain was happening to someone else. And for only a moment, she looked at them and felt new tears in her eyes.

Darkness was coming. It crept along the edges of her thoughts and blurred away the perimeter of her consciousness like the glow of the streetlights in reverse. Her body was no longer responding to anything she tried to tell it. Blood rolled down the back of her neck. Each blink felt long and heavy. Tears left a glaze of salty ice on her pale cheeks. One more breath before the nothingness carried with it a single word, a question she knew they would never answer.

"Why?"

The library was one of those places where you could lose yourself and no one would ever notice.

It wasn't empty. There were students hunched over the tables surrounded by books and notes. Others filled the corners, tucked away into the oblivion of research, their headphones firmly blocking out the world around them. Those up walking around went right by. Some even made brief, uncommitted eye contact. None noticed. None would even remember those moments later when they were trying to piece together every detail of what had happened.

That made it easy to walk through even the open area at the heart of the building and then into the stacks. No one took note of a book being drawn from the stack, the pages deliberately and strategically opened to a specific paragraph. There was no need to rush drawing out the glass vial and carefully underlining the words. A few soft breaths dried the blood enough to close the cover. The book was back on the shelves without a single other person even noticing it had been taken down. And there it would wait.

CHAPTER ONE

Callan Thorne

Nine years ago

I FELT THE GROUND SHAKE WHEN THE BUS STATION EXPLODED.
I heard the sound and thought a truck had hit the dumpster behind the student commons again. The radiating metallic sound of that impact didn't come, but I couldn't think of anything else it could be. Even when I saw the black smoke billowing into the sky and heard the sirens cutting through the constant murmur of campus, my brain wouldn't process that something truly horrific had actually happened.

The city was still new to me. I was a freshman. Not a "first year" the way some of the pretentious universities put it. Just a freshman. As in fresh from toppling off the heady pinnacle of senior year in high school right back to the bottom of the heap. At least in the urban university I'd set my sights on the last time I held that illustrious title, it didn't feel so much like being crushed under the weight of a hierarchy—one topped by a clique held together by money, lip gloss, and disdain for everyone whose shared history couldn't be traced back to elementary school. The concept of oral tradition took on a slightly different meaning when it applied to them however.

I was back at square one, but the years stretched out ahead of me felt full of opportunity rather than like I was about to run the gauntlet. That's one of the dirty little secrets of high school. There's an image of what people believe the social structure looks like and the people who are immune to the torment. In reality, almost no one gets out of there unscathed.

After graduation, I was blissfully happy to put all that bullshit behind me and see where starting something new in Richmond would bring me. Now, just a few months later, I was standing outside the library listening to the screams of other students around me, gradually coming to the realization that something really was wrong.

My life changed that day.

I wasn't naive. At least, I never would have described myself that way. I guess just about every kid thinks they know everything when they are that age. They've taken two steps beyond the threshold of childhood and are convinced they have it all figured out. It isn't until you've gone fully through that phase and are separated from it by a few years that you really start to realize just how much of the world was still the unknown. That day brought some of that recognition right to my feet.

Before that day, I never would have thought of myself as sheltered. I'd seen my fair share of tragedy play out on the internet and TV. But that day changed how I saw the world around me. Suddenly I realized just how distanced I really was from things like war and mass shootings that had once felt so close.

It was one thing to see the horrifying imagery and listen to eyewitness statements. It was something completely different to feel the ground move from the force of an explosion and smell the fire in the air. I didn't really realize I was running away from the library when my feet first started moving. People around me were streaming toward the other side of campus, and I got swept up into the current.

Sirens started coming from all different directions. Around me, overlapping voices in alternating shouts and whispers questioned what was happening or claimed in some sort of unsupported authority to already know.

"There's a shooter."

"Was it the science building? Did an experiment go wrong?"

"A truck lost control and crashed into one of the buildings up on Broad Street."

"Maybe someone was smoking and tossed their cigarette too close to the gas station."

"We're under attack. My friend just told me she saw a military helicopter."

No one actually knew what they were talking about. None of us knew what was going on because at the moment no one did.

It felt like the intention of the mob we'd formed was to walk down the center of Broad Street toward the smoke and the sound of the sirens and blaring horns. We would march like a demonstration, a protest against the confusion and fear we were feeling. But we didn't get far. Cars and buses congested the lanes. Police leaned out of their windows with the flash of their lights to shout at everyone to go home. Get inside. Your dorm. Your apartment. Don't go to class. Don't go get something to eat.

Go home.

But even with all of us being forced off the street and back to whatever we were choosing to call home at that particular moment, it didn't take long for me to find out what had happened. By the time I stepped into my dorm room, the news was on TV. My roommate and I sat on the edges of our individual beds, staring at the screen positioned directly between them, and watched as the bus station burned.

It was surreal watching the people running frantically around the parking lot and hordes of firefighters trying to beat back flames while others dug through rubble. It was one of those images that should have been happening across the world. Somewhere else. Not a couple of miles from where I was sitting.

I knew that bus station. Not that it had any kind of serious emotional weight to me at the time or anything, but I was familiar with it. I caught buses out of it a couple of times for weekend trips over the last few months I was in the city. And a bunch of us had gone to a game at the baseball stadium positioned directly across the street when we were feeling like getting more involved with our new community, so I remembered looking at it and wondering about the people moving in and out with their luggage. Some walked in with the determined stride of people who knew exactly where they were going and were only focused on getting there. Others had more of a meandering gait, like they weren't sure what was coming next but were hoping to get answers inside the cavernous building.

Then it was a center of activity. Buses rolling into the long row of bays. Workers scurrying around, making sure the schedule stayed on track.

Now it was a pile of debris and unstable remnants of walls. The news report showed a deluge of dirty water flooding the parking lot and brightly colored bits of fabric scattered among the chunks of concrete and fractured tile. Torn clothing from the people who were inside when the explosion happened.

At the time, that was the only way they could describe it. An explosion. No one had any idea what caused the blast that ripped through the building and started the death toll counting. The hopeful said maybe it was a gas leak or an electrical malfunction. The cynical said a terrorist attack. The fact that the police made us go back to our homes rather than continue to wander around campus or even go to class gave a hint to what side they were on.

Not knowing made it worse. Tension crept down the back of my neck and tightened the muscles along my shoulders. The palms of my hands tingled. I came to the university looking for a new experience. I wanted to know what it was like to meld into a city and be a part of something constantly thumping and thriving. I'd spent a good amount of time in Richmond but never lived there. I knew it was going to be different to fully become a part of it. The comparison between here and the suburb where I grew up was the difference between being the blood in someone's veins and the air in their lungs. I had a few ideas of what I might want to do with my life. That day sparked something inside me.

I watched the news voraciously every day after that. I craved every detail of the case as it unfolded. I started taking the city bus down to the street where the corpse of the station stood so I could watch what was happening around it. I sat on the grass in front of the baseball stadium, not realizing the hours that were passing. Finding out the explosion wasn't an accident or equipment failure but a purposeful, targeted attack made me all the more obsessed with witnessing it develop.

Then I saw her.

The week or so that had passed since the explosion had changed the area around the station. Where it had been blocked off for days so only police, emergency personnel, and contractors could go in, now it was starting to open up again. People were driving past with only a slight slowing of their pace or even none at all. They were used to it by now.

The blackened, crumbled heap and aching shell still occasionally crumbling was just another part of their landscape now.

The remains of the station itself had been surrounded by a security fence, and the strange dichotomy of moving forward had begun. While some of the crew still searched in protective body gear for victims, or the parts of them that hadn't yet been recovered from the rubble, others scooped away the rocks to clear the space so the teams coming in with suits, button-down shirts, and tablets in their hands could talk about rebuilding. Death, destruction, and healing existed all together in the same space, overlapping in the same moment.

That was what brought her there. I was standing where I usually did, eating the wax-paper-wrapped lunch I'd gotten from one of the food trucks that showed up in the area from time to time, and I noticed a black car slide into place in the section of parking lot that had somewhat gone undamaged. A woman climbed out of it and stood for a few seconds, just looking at the aftermath. She turned her head enough for me to see the dark sunglasses, which she wore to block out the same rays that shimmered on her blonde hair tied tight into a thick ponytail. A badge dangled from her neck, and when she walked toward the officer standing at the yellow tape blocking the way inside, she did it like she owned everything her black boots crossed.

I didn't realize immediately that I knew who she was. I'd heard her name on the news broadcasts I was devouring when they showed up on TV and when I hunted them down on the internet. Emma Griffin, Special Agent of the Federal Bureau of Investigation.

There had been talk about her getting involved in the case. She had personal ties to Richmond and was already known to have an upcoming case going through the courts in the city. She was going to be in town for as long as it took to testify in the twisted, grotesque case of a serial killer she nearly didn't survive the year before. People assumed that meant she would dip into at least consulting on the explosion that had been officially determined to be a targeted attack.

But that trial didn't start for another week, and nothing had been said about her arriving in the city. I was so focused on her that I barely noticed the man walking beside her until they walked up to a uniformed officer and he gestured like he was introducing Agent Griffin.

"Callan?"

I heard my name and turned toward it, seeing Tabitha—a friend from my history class—hurrying toward me. I'd spent far more time out there than I thought I had if she was rushing to get me so we could get to the lecture on time. She stopped beside me and shuddered when she looked at the station.

"Why do you keep coming out here? This is just depressing."

"Figuring out what I want to be when I grow up," I said, calling back a conversation we'd just had with some other friends over dinner at the dining hall.

"And what's that?" she asked.

I pointed across the street at Agent Griffin walking into the chaos.

"Her."

CHAPTER TWO

Emma

Now

I TAKE MY KNEE OUT OF THE MIDDLE OF THE MAN'S CHEST, STANDING up carefully to ensure he doesn't have enough space to get up from his prone position. Not that he has the will left in him to do it. I've made sure to break that in my chase. He thought he could just pick one of the bottom-of-the-barrel guys of his crime family to be his patsy and leave him behind like bait. He thought I would be fooled, or that at least we would put so much energy and attention on swarming that guy and trying to get all the information we could that he would be able to get away without a second thought.

I can't really blame him for thinking that. He's done similar things several times before. That's the whole reason I'm here. He's been able to duck the police task force one too many times, and he's been careless enough to leave a trail of crimes not only horrific, but that cross several state lines and involve people who aren't even old enough to vote in the next presidential election.

He isn't selling them. That has been his big defense. He isn't selling the teenagers, so the law needs to back off and take it easier on him. It doesn't matter that he is training an army of kids—who should have been planning for homecoming dances and trying to circumvent school dress codes instead of running drugs and attracting wealthy clients for the women and men he actually is selling.

That has all been a big misunderstanding.

And that's what I told him about my boot crushing into his spine and sending him onto his face when I caught up with him. It was all just a big misunderstanding. I would much rather have been looking into his face.

I step back and push my gun back into its holster as officers handcuff Will Joyner and drag him up to his feet. He stares at me like he wants to spit in my face. It wouldn't be the first time someone did that after I take them down. I'm glad he has refrained. I can handle a lot of things when it comes to scraping criminals off the underbelly of society, but dealing with spitefully inflicted bodily fluids is not among my favorites.

I'm exhausted by the time I get finished filling out the deluge of paperwork that comes with wrapping up a case and head for my car. The duffel bag tossed over my shoulder has my clothes from the chase and a toiletry kit that dearly needs replenishing after several weeks of near-constant traveling for my recent cases. Joyner might not have spit on me, but I get back to the office coated in sweat and grit and am thankful for fifteen minutes spent under a stream of high-pressure water. First blisteringly hot and then a blast of cold.

"You headed out?" Quinn, the security guard, asks as I walk to the front door.

"Absolutely, before they figure out I've had enough time to breathe and decide to throw me into something else," I say. "It's been a hell of a… month? Season?"

"Lifetime?" Quinn asks.

I laugh and nod.

"Run."

"Unfortunately, these people are trained too. Especially with how beaten up I got chasing Joyner through that factory he turned into the damn ghetto Taj Mahal, I think they'll be able to catch me if they want me," I say.

"Emma, run."

Quinn's voice has changed. There's no humor in it now. I notice his eyes have moved over my shoulder and are locked on the hallway behind me. His hand has moved to his hip, a gesture I know well. He's reaching for his gun. Somewhere in the recesses of the building, I hear a strange rhythmic sound. I turn and step backward at the same time to put more space between myself and whatever he's looking at. It's late, so many of the lights in the building have been turned off, leaving the hallway shrouded in shadows.

It isn't dark enough to conceal the figure standing there.

Tall and shapeless under a flowing black robe with the hood pulled up so it casts a deeper shadow on the white mask beneath, the figure looks straight out of a slasher film. Right down to the knife they slowly pull from their pocket.

The high-pitched sound continues as Quinn takes a step across the small entryway where he usually sits behind his security desk if he's not prowling the building. His hand is gripping his gun now, ready to withdraw it if he needs to. He can't just shoot. He wants to. And yet he doesn't. I can see both in the way his body is positioned and the look on his face. If this really were one of the gory movies Dean has a particular taste for and that I can't ever look at the same way after my attack in August, Quinn would have just whipped out his gun and emptied it toward the figure the second he saw it.

But that isn't how it works in reality. We can't react to everything with the pull of a trigger.

I step closer, putting myself in the space between Quinn and the figure.

"Who are you?" I demand.

The figure lifts the knife higher and takes a stride forward. In an instant, I toss my bag to the side and pull out my own gun, training it directly on the ridiculous robe. The fact that this person is dressed in a costume makes me angry. I hate the games. I hate the theatrics.

"Put the knife down and back up," I shout.

Quinn has already moved around the desk to call 911, but I don't back down. I'm not afraid.

I take another step, and the figure suddenly shifts, turning to the side and running down the other hallway. I take off after them and hear the elevator door closing. The repetitive dinging sound has stopped, and

I realize it's the alarm meant to alert that the elevator door is being held open. The doors are already closed by the time I get down the hallway.

"They put something in the elevator doors to stop them from closing," I tell Quinn. "They're headed upstairs."

"The police will be here in a couple of minutes," he tells me.

"They can meet me up there," I say, already pushing through the door to the stairwell.

He's calling after me, but his voice is muffled by the sound of the door closing behind me. I don't know which floor the elevator stopped, so I move carefully when I get to the landings. There are no windows in the doors blocking each floor from the stairs, and they are too thick to hear through clearly, especially someone walking on carpet and who likely doesn't want to be heard. I can only assume the figure went higher than the first floor past the lobby, and there are only three other floors, so I run until I reach the top floor.

Whoever this person is knows I'm following them. There's no other reason for them to block the elevator doors from closing and get in it as soon as they see me starting after them. If they were trying to escape, they would simply go through the emergency door at the very end of the hallway. However they got into the building, they've done it with the intention of letting me see them and pursuing. I know that, but it doesn't make me any less willing to do it.

The costume and the drama of their appearance tell me there's more to them showing up here than hurting someone. They want to be seen. They want to be chased. That doesn't mean they are necessarily not dangerous. If there's any chance they could have intended to hurt someone, I have to be there to try to stop them. Even if it is putting myself in their path. It's likely the very reason they are doing it this way. So that I will come after them.

The question is what they have planned for me now that I've complied.

I get to the top floor and step to the side so that when I turn the knob and fling the door open, I'm not directly in front of the open space. There's nothing there, and I step into the hallway, my gun in front of me. The rows of offices are closed and dark. In another hour or so, the cleaning crew will arrive, but for now this part of the building is quiet. When I was heading for the shower, everyone else was heading out, leaving what I thought was just Quinn and me. It means whoever this person is knows the building is empty. It also means whatever sound I hear shouldn't be there.

I go through the top floor and find nothing. The elevator is empty and still. I go down the steps to the next floor and repeat the process. Through a window at the end of the hall, I see the flashing of police cars pouring into the parking lot. I go to the next floor and hear the sound of a door slamming at the end of the hallway. Chasing after it, I see what looks like someone curled up on the floor. Getting closer, I see it's just the black robe and mask.

The door to the stairwell behind me slams open.

"Agent Griffin," a voice shouts. "Are you all right?"

I turn to look over my shoulder at the impending clutch of officers. I lift up the mask and show it to them.

"I'm fine. Looks like someone just missed the memo that Halloween was over more than two months ago," I say.

"Keeping the spirit alive," another of the officers says, his eyes sparkling with the joke until a scathing glare from his superior wipes the expression away.

"Just a prank," I say, getting to my feet and handing the mask to the officer at the front of the group, a man I know as Rob Purcell. "We might want to find out how whoever it was managed to get in here. Unless it was one of the guys thinking he was being funny."

Purcell takes one look at the mask and scoffs. "At least they could have gone with something a little more original."

"I don't think he was aiming for awards season," I say.

My gun is already in my holster, and I head for the steps.

"What should we do with this stuff?" one of the officers calls after me.

"Doesn't matter to me," I say. "Does the barracks have a dress-up room?"

They laugh, and I wave as I head down the stairs to the lobby. Quinn is standing with another officer, and his eyes widen when he sees me.

"Emma, what happened?" he asks.

"Nothing," I tell him. "Whoever it was is gone. I found the robe and mask in the hallway upstairs. I'm guessing they went out through the emergency exit while you were talking to the officers."

"I would have seen it if somebody did that," he protests.

"Are you suggesting he disappeared?" I ask.

His eyes lift to the ceiling.

"If he's still in the building, the officers will find him. But my guess is, he knew we were both distracted and slipped out. Just somebody who thinks they're really funny."

THE GIRL AND THE SECRET PASSAGE

Sam isn't as sure about that explanation when I tell him about the encounter when I finally make it home. I'm so tired I know I probably should have stopped at a hotel rather than tacking another hour onto my day to get home, but I couldn't stand the thought of another night in a hotel away from my husband. I've been away from home more than enough these last several weeks. The holidays only made it harder, though I am glad I at least got the chance to celebrate Christmas with my family. I was back on the road just a couple days later, and I feel like I've barely stopped since.

But Sam isn't sweeping me into his arms and spinning me around in a traditional romantic greeting. He pops up at the front door before I even get out of my car and questions me about the man as I am walking toward him. Purcell has ratted me out.

I'm not surprised. Law enforcement runs tight around here, even when not in the same town. And when a sheriff is married to an FBI agent with a propensity for attracting a full range of attention through her cases, the other officers in the vicinity take notice.

"It was a prank, Sam," I say, walking past him to go into the kitchen.

I take a glass down out of the kitchen cabinet. It's one of those moments when I realize it won't be too much longer that I will call this house "home." Pretty soon the renovations and improvements on the house Sam grew up in will be finished, and he and I will move the few blocks away to start a new chapter there. Dean and Xavier will take over living here in the house my grandmother decorated and my grandfather repaired countless times. The house where I have so many memories of Christmas, Easter, Thanksgiving, and birthdays.

But it's because of those memories that I'm ready to finish packing up the cardboard boxes already stashed around the house and leave them for Dean to discover. Those memories are rightfully his too. He just doesn't have them. He's never had the chance to make them. I know signing over the deed to him won't give him back the years he's never had with the family. It won't make him know our grandparents or my mother. But at least it's a chance for him to have more of a connection to them, and it also gives them space of their own here in Sherwood so they can spread out and relax more when they are in town.

It was an extremely emotional moment when we handed over the papers and explained the plan. It was strange because while I was actually living that moment with them, I felt like it wasn't the first time. I had been in that scenario before. During the sharp lucid dreams of my coma, I lived that moment, knowing it was what I wanted to do and then giving it to them. Only, then there wasn't anything that needed to be done at Sam's parents' house and we were able to celebrate Christmas at both homes.

I haven't asked Xavier about that part of the dream. I already know the other dreams were because he was sitting up beside me telling me stories, detailing the cases they were able to solve by going through my notes. All but the final, most chilling of my dreams. That one he concocted as a way to bring me at least close to knowing his sister—a woman who, even for Xavier, lives in a shadowy realm somewhere between reality and imagination.

I don't know if he planted the suggestion for the house or if it was just my thoughts of entering into unexplored corners of my brain while it had the uninterrupted time because I was unconscious. It doesn't really matter. Either way, it is exactly what should be.

"How can you possibly call that a prank?" Sam asks, ruining the hazy nostalgic moment I was drifting away into.

I sigh, rolling my eyes as I close the cabinet and bring the glass over to fill with water. Leaning back against the counter, I take a long sip. I would really like a cup of coffee right now, but I need to get some sleep.

"Because whoever it was had on a Halloween costume. And not even a good one. One of those cheap ones that feels a little like a parachute. I'll admit it was a little creepy looking down the hallway and seeing them standing there with the knife, but they didn't get anywhere near me. They didn't charge or stand around a corner. There wasn't any heavy breathing or creepy piano music going on behind me," I say.

"I'm glad you can joke about this," Sam says. "But you'll have to forgive me for still remembering what it was like to stand in the hospital room and look down at you, not knowing if you were going to survive."

I put my glass in the dishwasher and cross the room to him. Placing my hands flat on his chest, I lean back so I can look into his eyes.

"Babe, listen to me. I know where your brain is right now. Trust me, mine is too. I just don't want to let it be. I don't want to have to think about whoever this person is. I don't want to have to remember getting attacked in the living room or the fact that I was almost killed in the hospital. I don't want to think about the car chases. I don't want to think about any of it. I just want to say it was somebody playing a tasteless joke and go get some sleep," I say.

"Okay," he whispers, sounding slightly defeated. "But we're going to talk about this in the morning."

I have no doubt that we will. The truth has come out. As flippant and carefree as I'm trying to be, I don't really feel it. Seeing that person standing in the hallway and watching them come toward me, even just that one step, brought everything that's happened with my anonymous attacker right back to the forefront of my mind, and I haven't been able to shake it since.

Whoever it is has been quiet for a while. I haven't experienced anything I can attribute to them since they prevented a serial killer from getting to me in the dark parking lot just before Halloween, then left me a note to make sure I was aware they were the ones responsible. Since then, they've stayed away—or at least, not made themselves known. It isn't that I've forgotten about them, but I've been trying not to sink back into my obsession with my case. But now I'm forced to focus on it again.

I know the people in my life think I should just leave it to those around me who are fighting for me. I know the investigation is still happening and that everybody wants me to feel safe because they are doing everything they can. And I have been investigating and fighting right along beside them. But I can't just act like my attacker doesn't impact every moment of my life. This person's mere existence is like a vein of poison through everything I do. Even when I'm trying with everything in me not to think about them, it's always in the back of my mind. I'm always wondering when the next time will be that I find something they've left for me. When I will look in my rearview mirror and see a car speeding toward me to force me off the road. When they will finally come back to my home or a hotel where I'm staying and try to finish what they started.

I've gone over several options for who it may be. I've researched all the people I think could be responsible, tracking down criminals I put in jail, finding out what has come of the crime families I've broken up. I've done everything I can think of, but I still haven't been able to narrow it down to anyone I really think it could be.

I go to bed that night with a thought swirling into the edge of my mind like smoke. A thought I've had a few times before and immediately shoved down. But I can't sleep. I stare up at the ceiling, and I wonder if it's my only option.

Maybe I should go talk to Anson.

I have visited him in prison before to talk about other cases, but it isn't something I want to do again. I don't want to create a bond with him or have him think that he is important to me in some way. That's what got us into trouble to begin with. But at the same time, he might have insight into this that no one else can give me. After all, he's did so much of the same thing. He came after me. He stalked and harassed me. He tried to kill me on several occasions. Maybe he can look at it in a different way and help me find a way to the person who seems to have taken up Anson's sword.

My absolute exhaustion drags me into sleep before I've made any decision, and the next thing I'm aware of is the sharp trill of my phone cutting through the emptiness of dreamless sleep. I don't want to answer it. I want to throw it into the hallway, roll over, and keep sleeping until I've caught up on the several days' worth I feel like I've missed.

It doesn't work out that way.

After the first series of rings ends, another starts up immediately. Whoever is calling is insistent. Which is very rarely a good thing. When I finally grab my phone and look at it, I see Eric's name on the screen. My stomach sinks. Usually, that wouldn't be the reaction to one of my best friends calling, but when that best friend is also my boss, and knows very well to text if I'm not answering and he just wants to chat, it hits differently.

"Hey," I say, rolling onto my back and forcing myself to sit up. "What's up?"

"I need you to get to Richmond," he says.

"Richmond?" I groan. "Why? I just got home."

"An agent was seriously injured in the field and can't continue her investigation. I need you to take over for her."

CHAPTER THREE

"Her name is Callan Thorne. She's young and new to the Bureau, just a few years in, but she's showing a lot of promise. That's why I had her take the lead on this one. But it went bad, and now she's in the hospital, being kept under in hopes her body will heal and she'll survive."

Shit. That sounds familiar.

"What's the case?" I ask.

"Possible serial killer on and around the campus," he says.

The words burst in my head. "Campus? My campus?"

It isn't really my school. I've taken a few classes there and gone back a few times for intensives and workshops, but it isn't the university I graduated from. But I still maintain a close attachment to the school and my time there. It hasn't been immune to horrific things happening there, and I don't want to think about another person coming and wreaking havoc on the students.

"Yeah. Look, I don't have all the details. I just need you to get there as fast as you can. I've already spoken with the local detective who's been on the investigation since the beginning. She'll give you all the details," Eric says.

"Where is Agent Thorne? Is she in the hospital there in the city?" I ask.

"Yes. We didn't have her transferred," he says.

"I'll get there this afternoon," I tell him.

I get out of bed and head right for the shower. The hot water wakes me up, and I'm dressed and in the kitchen by the time Sam comes out of the home gym he's made out of one of the extra bedrooms. He looks at me like he's surprised to see me.

"I didn't think you'd be up," he says. "You didn't get much sleep."

"And it doesn't look like I'm going to be getting any more right now. I just got off the phone with Eric. I've got to go to Richmond," I tell him.

I fill him in on what Eric told me. Concern flickers across Sam's face. I know it isn't all for the injured agent or even the victims of the crime she's been investigating. He doesn't like the idea of me traveling again so soon, especially with the issue of the costumed person from last night still unresolved. But he also knows this is my job. I'm not just choosing to venture off on a whim. Eric needs me on this case, so I have to go.

"How long do you think you'll be gone?" he asks, following me and my massive cup of coffee back into the bedroom so I can start packing.

"You know I can't answer that," I tell him. "I don't even know all the details about the case yet. But I'll do my best. I hope I'm able to solve it and get home soon."

Sam walks over and kisses me. "Me too."

Rather than taking the time to eat, I call ahead to Pearl's and order breakfast that I can pick up and eat on the road. From the way Eric described the case, this sounds like an active and imminently dangerous situation. I don't have even seconds to waste. Callan has already been investigating. I'm already at a disadvantage and chasing after everything she's done. I need to get there and get up to date as fast as possible.

It's early afternoon by the time I get to the hospital in Richmond. The people at the information desk have already been given notification that I am on my way, so my identification badge is ready, and they don't bat an eye when I sweep through the doors and ask to be shown to Callan Thorne's room.

I don't even know her, but it's still gut-wrenching when I walk in and see her lying on a bed connected to so many tubes and wires. She looks small and vulnerable. I know she's well into adulthood. Eric has told me she's twenty-seven, the same age I was when I faced down Jake Logan in Feathered Nest. But she seems so young. I feel instantly protective of her.

Aware of still being a total stranger to her, I stand back away from the bed but watch the screen behind her that records her heartbeat and one on the other side that monitors her blood pressure. The steady, soft beep beneath the quiet of her deep sleep is reassuring. Her vitals are stable. It's incredibly hard to see her like this. The medically induced coma is a critical protective measure. It ensures her body isn't fighting against itself or focusing energy on tasks beyond mending the damage so clearly done to her. She has bruises and cuts across her face and her arms. Her hands show obvious signs of defense. She didn't go down gently. Whoever came for her got a battle. I wouldn't be surprised to find out they didn't think they left her alive.

Those evident injuries standing out so garishly against the crisp white backdrop of the hospital bedding and the unnatural stillness of her sedated body also bring up the difficult emotions linked to my own, so very similar experience not long ago. Less than five months ago, I was in her position, lying in a Sherwood hospital bed with medication keeping me asleep and machines making sure I was still alive.

I've been grappling with my feelings about my own experience, but seeing her like this underscores the struggle of what it means to go through this kind of pain and difficulty in the name of your career. It's worth it. I will never say it isn't, no matter what. There isn't a single injury or challenge I would say is too much to put myself through because it is all for the purpose of what I am meant to do: be an agent.

At the same time, it can be nothing short of terrifying. I never want to say that out loud. There have been very few times in all the years I've been with the Bureau that I actually have admitted to it. I do my best to keep all that in, to insulate myself against it and force myself to think only of my end goal. But it's still there. Every time I walk through a crime scene, I can feel the violence and horror of that crime burned into the atmosphere. I carry the victims with me and take on their suffering. There are times when it is daunting.

It's different for me now. I am far into my career, more than a decade behind my badge, and I have been through a tremendous amount in that time. I've come to—if not accept the horrors that come along with it—at least be more prepared for them. I know what's possible and what is in me to handle it. But this girl is so young and hasn't gone through nearly as much. To have this happen to her only a few years into her career, just like my time in Feathered Nest, is horrifying.

Looking at her and seeing myself alongside her makes me protective and angry. This is a young woman who has committed her life to other people. She has offered herself up, quite literally, to try to protect the lives of people she would otherwise have never encountered. And it has brought her here. Whoever she has been hunting is still out there. I'm going to find them.

This ends with me. I will not only finish the case, but I will get justice for Callan as well.

"She looks better."

I turn around and see a man only a couple of years older than Callan standing just inside the doorway. He takes a cautious step toward me and extends his hand.

"Agent Griffin, it's a pleasure and an honor to meet you. I'm Callan's partner."

CHAPTER FOUR

I TAKE HIS HAND AND SHAKE IT, LIFTING ONE EYEBROW AT HIM.

"Her partner…?" I prompt.

"In the Bureau," he clarifies. "I am working with her on this investigation."

I nod. "Agent Blanchard. Eric Martinez told me to get in touch with you. I guess you're doing that for me."

He gives a nod in return. "I just left for a couple of hours, I wanted to make sure she's all right. Please, call me Jackson."

"Jackson," I say, "I'm sorry you're having to go through something like this. Seeing your partner this way is incredibly difficult."

"It is." He looks at her with an expression that's hard to read. I can't really place the emotion in his eyes or the hard expression on his young face.

"Have you known her long?" I ask.

The question brings his attention back to me, and he shakes his head. It looks partly like he's answering me and partly like he's trying to get rid of thoughts that made it past his defenses.

"No. Not really. I've only worked with her really briefly on one other case."

There's a dismissiveness to the comment, like it is his way of telling me they don't have much of a bond. I know as well as anyone that regardless of whether you consider the people you work with as friends, or whatever kind of closeness you may feel with them, any time you work on an investigation with someone, there is a connection.

"She seems better than I expected," I say. "At least it seems they have stabilized her."

Jackson is looking at her again and gives a slight nod without saying anything. The muscles at the side of his jaw twitch, but I don't think it's sadness coming to the surface. Instead, he looks tense and frustrated.

"Why are you here?" he suddenly asks. "I'm sorry. I know that was really rude. I just… Why are you here?"

There it is. He isn't frustrated at what happened to Callan. He's frustrated I'm here.

"I'm sure you know Agent Martinez assigned me to take over the case, considering Agent Thorne is no longer capable of carrying on with the investigation," I say.

"Yes, I know that. It's why I'm asking. Like I just told you, I'm Callan's partner on this investigation. I've been alongside her since we first got the case. I know you are an incredible agent, Agent Griffin, and I truly do give you all due respect, but I don't understand why someone from the outside needed to be brought in when I could handle it the rest of the way myself," he says.

All the aggravation tumbles out of him, overshadowing his worry about Callan with his own offense at not being trusted to take on the case by himself now that she has been taken out of the equation. It's obvious he feels that I am stepping on his toes, but I don't feel the need to apologize or even to try to comfort him. This is basic reality when you're in the Bureau. He isn't miffed because a coworker is chosen over him to bake somebody's birthday cake; this is a multiple-murder situation.

I am by far his senior both in age and experience. This case is already one that requires more than one person managing it. Now it is even more pressing that it be brought under control and the person stopped.

"This case has proven very difficult and dangerous. Callan was severely injured and could have died if she wasn't found when she was. Do you know who committed these murders?" I ask.

Jackson stares back at me for a few seconds, then gives his head a hard shake. "No."

"Then there is more investigation ahead, and it's not going to get easier or safer now that there's an agent lying in a hospital bed. She didn't end up here because she slipped and fell. Someone did this to her, and it looks like they wanted her dead. This is not a case to be taken lightly, and you should not be doing it on your own. Agent Martinez called me in because he knows me and my skills well. He believes I can step in and help bring this case to a close. That should be the priority right now," I say.

Jackson swallows hard and looks like he's fighting to hold his composure together.

"That *is* my priority," he tells me in a low, controlled tone.

"Good. Then we're on the same page," I say. "I'm going to talk to the doctor and then to the police station. You have my contact information?"

"Yes."

"I'll be in touch."

My conversation with the doctor is brief and doesn't give me a lot of information. Because Callan is an adult and I don't have any specific permission from her to know her private medical information, the doctor's hands are tied a bit in terms of what he's able to share with me. He could tell me she was found in the canal and suffered a fairly extensive list of injuries. They were very worried about her when she first came in, unsure if she was going to be able to pull through, but she has since been responding well to treatment, and they are far more confident now.

That's a relief, though I know just because she's doing well now doesn't guarantee she will continue to improve. I can still so distinctly remember the intense roller coaster I went on while Greg was in intensive care right after resurfacing following a two-year disappearance. It was such an incredible relief that he was alive and I finally knew where he was—even if I didn't have answers as to where he had gone or what happened to him during those two years. I wasn't prepared for the emotional turmoil that came from him responding to treatments and experiencing incremental improvements in his condition, which were almost immediately followed by crashes and unexplainable setbacks like infections.

Callan's injuries are nowhere near as extensive and horrific as Greg's, so I can only hope she will continue to improve.

I leave the hospital and drive through the city, down toward campus. This is one of the few times when I'm glad for stoplights. I love the opportunity to slow down in this area and look at the buildings. Many of them are the unappealing, bland gray cement of contemporary urban expansion, but tucked in among them are buildings dating back more than a century that give Richmond a unique flavor I've never really experienced anywhere else.

One of my favorites is a part of the sprawling medical complex taking up a good portion of the city. Known as the Egyptian Building, it strikes many who venture past it as an odd little flight of whimsy, I'm sure. As if it was built in fairly recent times when the art and alternative scenes really exploded throughout the city. The fact that such an explanation couldn't be further from the truth just makes me love it even more. In reality, the Egyptian Building was completed in the 1840s as the home of a medical college, then changed hands many decades later.

I leave the bustling professional area and venture closer to the university campus and residential areas. I feel very comfortable here, and there are times when I look back on the brief snippets of time I spent here and wish I hadn't changed my mind about where I wanted to go to school. My college experience was great, but I never had quite the same kind of feeling at the University of Alexandria as I did here. Richmond is a city that speaks to me. Before the thought of joining the FBI even crossed my mind, I was on the path toward being an artist. I brought that with me when I changed schools, but I know the artsy vibe of this place would have been such a better fit for me.

As I park in one of the countless decks dotting the city streets and start out on foot, my mind sifts through all the ways my life could have changed if I had come here full time. Sam and I never would have broken up as teenagers. I wouldn't have Eric and Bellamy. It would have been a completely different life.

I stuff my hands down my pockets and duck my head into the biting-cold early January wind.

But this is the one I chose, and I'm going to do everything I can with it.

I leap onto the sidewalk across the street and continue on toward the police station where I'm meeting with the detective who started the investigation. With dorms and the park behind me, this is the outskirts of campus. Most of the time people venturing this way are heading toward the nightclubs several blocks down or stopping by one of the little restaurants nestled among larger buildings—easy to miss if you don't know just what you are looking for, but generally the most amazing food available in the city. I breathe in the smell of one of them. A rich, deep smell of garlic and warm fresh bread emanates from the tiny family-owned pizza shop not far from where I'm walking.

My breakfast from Pearl's was several hours ago, but I'm still full. Maybe I'll grab a few slices to bring back to the hotel with me once I'm done talking to the detective. A loud sound behind me makes me turn and look over my shoulder, but I don't see anyone around who looks like they are paying any attention to me being there. It's not a surprise. A woman in a suit with a long, black jacket and with her hair slicked back into a ponytail doesn't exactly stand out in a place like this, where there is always more than enough to look at. That's exactly the way I want it to be.

CHAPTER FIVE

Callan Thorne

Two weeks ago

I TURNED BACK AROUND FROM GLANCING OVER MY SHOULDER toward the sound of squealing tires, relieved that the driver of the car seemingly losing control was able to get it back before they smashed into anything. The last thing the city needed right now was a horrific vehicle accident. I filled my lungs with the smell of freshly baked pizza from a little spot not far up the road. I had ventured up this way to get pizza in the middle of the night what felt like a thousand times during college and in the years after. Maybe I would grab some for lunch later, but for now I was expected at the police department.

I buzzed with anticipation and pent-up energy as I walked toward the door. This was the first time I would lead a major case like this. Only a few years out from graduating from the Academy, I still felt like I was proving myself. Being handed an active serial killer was both an affirmation and a test. I had proven myself enough to even come up for consideration and taking on the case, but there was also an element of feeling like I was being carefully evaluated in every step I took to gauge just how I was going to react to the challenges and pressures of being at the lead of a fast-moving, deadly situation.

This wasn't a cold case. It wasn't the FBI looking into bones that had been discovered or killings that had stopped months before. This was happening now. The bodies still were not yet in the ground, and the city was like a pressure cooker waiting for another.

Despite the fact that I was young and still, in the greater scheme of things, at the beginning of my career, I felt like this case belonged to me. This was my city, my home. It infuriated me to think of someone prowling the streets and turning them into their own personal hunting ground. I had been tasked with finding out who they were and stopping them, and that was exactly what I intended to do.

I wasn't doing it on my own. At least, not in theory. I was supposed to be working with Jackson Blanchard. I had only worked with him on one other case and wasn't quite sure about him yet. In reality, I didn't want a partner at all. I wished I could just work these cases alone. I didn't like the idea of having to report to someone else, having to explain my actions, or being held back by someone, even a person with more experience in the Bureau than me.

Even though I understood the concept of safety and protocol, I much preferred to rely on and trust myself rather than having to think about another person while investigating. It was easier to sink into my own thoughts and let them guide me rather than having to piece them together into language consumable by someone else and wait for approval. On this point though, it seemed like I was functionally getting my desire. As soon as I got in touch with him, Jackson told me he wouldn't be available for the initial briefing with the detective but would meet up with me after so we could go over the information and devise our strategy.

This pissed me off right from the beginning. I was forced to have a partner but was apparently going to have to deal with a flippant, dismissive level of commitment. Despite the bristling reaction to Jackson's immediate failure in my eyes, I was determined to tolerate him and the situation so I could do exceptionally well in the case and continue to build my reputation in the Bureau. I wanted to climb out of what sometimes felt like a little glass box where I was constantly scrutinized by people who didn't believe in me and were just waiting for me to fail. I wanted to rise above that and show who I really was. With Emma Griffin as my idol, I had a lot to live up to. I was willing to do what it took to get there.

I walked into the police department and was immediately greeted by a tall, dark-skinned woman with expressive eyes but a tight, hardened jaw.

"Detective Monique Tarrant," the woman said, extending her hand to shake mine. "I'm the lead detective on this investigation. It's nice to meet you."

This woman had the kind of energy that seemed like she was always moving. Even when she was standing still, the electricity coming off her made it seem like something was about to happen.

"Agent Callan Thorne," I said, introducing myself. "Good to meet you."

The detective was already moving toward a door leading to the back of the building. I fell into step beside her. We went to a conference room where papers were waiting on a table, and Detective Tarrant gestured toward the chairs.

"Have a seat. Can I get you some coffee?"

I wasn't one to turn down a couple of shots of espresso early in the morning, but as a regular habit, I was far more of a tea drinker. Considering I doubted the department was well equipped with either, I just nodded.

"That would be great, thanks."

The detective walked out of the room and came back a few moments later carrying two mugs of coffee and a handful of sugar and cream packets. She set them down on the table in front of me and dropped a disdainful look at the little packages of plastic and paper.

"The department is trying to be more sustainable by encouraging us to use these mugs or travel tumblers when we're heading out instead of Styrofoam cups. But then they still have massive, compound-size boxes of these individual serving things stuffed into the cabinets of the lounge. Doesn't seem like a very good look," she said.

I shrugged and reached for several of the tiny tubs of creamer. "I guess this is one of those every- little-bit-helps kind of situations."

The detective snorted like she wasn't fully convinced by that explanation but would go with it. Taking her own cup, she sat down and dumped three packets of sugar into it. Swirling it around rather than stirring, she took a gulp, then added another packet of sugar.

"What do you know so far?" she asked.

"Just the basic details. A couple of victims, seemingly unrelated to each other. No particular leads."

"Those are definitely the basics." Detective Tarrant pulled a folder toward me across the table and flipped open the front cover to show a crime scene photo. "This is Warren Mason. Thirty-three. Four days ago, he was found in his apartment in the Museum District. There was absolutely nothing to go on at the scene or in his life according to the people we spoke with. He lived in one of the historic buildings, and there is no surveillance equipment in the area. None of his neighbors had anything to say about, it and there was nowhere to go with it.

"The next day we got a call from the library at the university. One of the librarians found a book that had been tampered with. A passage had been underlined in what looked like blood. When questioned about it further, she remembered a student who had checked out that book specifically showed her that a section of a page had been torn out before taking it. He wanted to make sure she noted it so he wouldn't be held responsible for the damage. That book was returned the day before the blood was found.

"We aren't sure what, if anything, the books have to do with the murder, but the timing seemed significant. So we took samples of the blood to be DNA tested. Later that day, another book was turned in with a section torn out of it. There's no way of knowing when it was done. Then, later, a second body was found. This time a student." Detective Tarrant flipped open another of the folders to show a grizzly image of a young woman lying dead in an alleyway.

"Danielle Scherer. She was a grad student at the university. Well loved, successful. She was on the fast track to something exceptional."

"Then she was found dead in an alley," I muttered.

"Officially, the cause of death was stabbing, but there was also blunt-force trauma like her head had been crushed down into the ground before the actual stabbing. The next morning, another book was found with a section underlined in blood," she said.

I pulled the folder closer to look more carefully at the meager amount of evidence that had been gathered so far. "And that was yesterday?"

"Yes. Initial investigations and crime scene evaluation didn't turn up any leads or viable clues. No fiber evidence. No fingerprints. Whoever did this has managed to completely avoid security systems, and it didn't leave us anything to even really get started on an investigation. Other than finding out more about the victims themselves, there hasn't been much we've been able to do. And we got the results back and sure enough, the first set of blood was from Warren Mason. The second we got the results, we called up the FBI. And since we don't know who did this or why, we can't be sure there isn't going to be another victim."

"That's why I'm here," I told her.

CHAPTER SIX

I was finally able to meet up with Jackson Blanchard an hour after my conversation with Detective Tarrant. We ended up going right back to the same conference room to escape the cold outside and ensure no one would overhear our discussion of the case. While talk of the bodies had already started to spread through the city, we wanted to do everything we could to keep the details close and protect the integrity of the investigation as much as possible.

"So we're spending our time looking at books?" Jackson said after I laid out everything.

"If that's what we have to do," I confirmed. "DNA results haven't come in for the second set of blood yet, but we do know that the first victim's blood was smeared on the pages. That sounds like a signature to me."

"Hrm," was all he responded with.

Jackson picked up his phone and looked at it, set it down on the table, then picked it up again. He had seemed distracted from the moment he walked into the room, and it was starting to feel obvious I was going to be largely on my own in this investigation. It was exactly what I wanted, but it was still frustrating. I didn't want to be sitting there in the conference room talking over what I had just found out from the detective. I wanted to be out in the city talking to people and trying to find more information.

It was there. It was always there. No matter how well a killer was able to cover their tracks. No matter how much effort went into stopping little connections from being made, the information was there. It was just a matter of finding it. And I didn't feel like I was going to find anything stuck in this beige room with a partner who seemed like he would rather be anywhere else.

"Something else more important than this?" I asked.

He at least had the decency to look uncomfortable as he set the phone to the side and refocused on her.

"No. What about the passages? What did they say?" he asked.

"The blood wasn't fully dry when the books were closed, so the blood spread a little. But if you look at them, you can see where the line is more distinct, so it's easier to detect the specific passage. Unfortunately, the books with the torn-out pages aren't quite as easy. There are just sections ripped out. No indication of which words were actually being removed."

"They didn't find the ripped-out sections?" Jackson asked.

"No. Which means we need to find identical editions of the books. Every version of a book printed has different layouts, which means there isn't going to be consistency from one version to another on what is printed on any given page. We have to find exact copies so we can try to figure out what these sections were," I told him.

The books themselves were being held in evidence, so I wasn't able to bring those with me to the bookstore, but Detective Tarrant had provided me with pictures of the books so I could easily compare them. The version in the bookstores was not the same as the one in the libraries, making the comparison more difficult. We were finally able to locate copies of the books in another library, but a new challenge presented itself.

"How are we supposed to know which words?" Jackson asked. "In both of these books, the sections that were ripped out have words on both sides of the paper. Which ones are the ones that they wanted to point out?"

I set the books down on the conference room table next to pictures of the damaged pages. The photographs were taken close enough to show the exact place where each of the pages had been torn. I took the books they had removed from the library with permission from the librarian and scanned the front and back of the pages that corresponded with the torn ones. Then I printed out the resulting images and used a pen to recreate the tear line where the section was separated from the rest of the page.

"If you look at the blood underlining in the other books, it's sharp. Super distinct. Yes, it was wet, and some of it soaked into the paper in other places, but that's just little specks. You can really see where whoever this was it took some sort of pointed instrument, maybe even a fountain tip pen dipped in the blood, and used it to precisely indicate these specific words."

"But then they just tore out pieces of paper," Jackson said.

"I don't think it was just tearing them out," I said. "This was for a reason. But what I'm saying is, they wanted to make sure whoever found these books knew what words to read. They were going to see that underline in blood, and it would be obvious those were the words making up whatever message they're trying to put across. Which means they weren't going to just haphazardly tear the paper and possibly damage the words that they wanted read."

"So?" Jackson asked.

I picked up the pen again and began crossing out words that were partially torn. "So these words can be eliminated. They are ripped, which means they wouldn't have the attention on them that this killer would want. I'm also going to say they wouldn't pull out pieces of sentences. Both of the passages that were underlined in blood are complete thoughts. Specific quotes. It isn't just a random assortment of words."

I crossed out the partial sentence at the top of the page. Flipping the paper over, I repeated the process. When I was done, I picked up a highlighter.

"There isn't much of any significance happening on the other side of the page. I think these are the right words."

I swept the vibrant green ink across the words.

"What do they mean?" Jackson asked with a frustrated sigh. "And what does any of this have to do with the murders, Thorne?"

"Just bear with me, okay?" I replied.

I looked down at the highlighted words and the images of the passages underlined in blood in the other books. I knew there was a possibility the words didn't mean anything at all. For all we knew, this meant nothing. Maybe the killer had simply left these clues for the fun of leaving trails of false clues that didn't end up having anything to do with how to solve the crimes.

Not only was it an effective diversionary tactic to derail a case and stop us from getting anywhere near the person responsible, it was also probably something fun for the killer to watch. They liked seeing how much they could manipulate us.

That meant it was possible that this person had come up with this entire book angle just to amuse themselves and distract from the actual killings. But I didn't think so. These words were significant. They were left there for a reason. I just didn't know yet what they meant.

"Why leave the books in the library though? The first victim wasn't even a student at the school," I said.

"Wasn't the second one?" Jackson asked.

"Yes. She was a graduate student. She finished her undergrad here too. But Warren Mason had no tangible links to the university as far as anyone has been able to find. He didn't work on campus. He wasn't dating a student or faculty. He lived close to the campus where quite a few students do, but so do thousands of other people who also have nothing to do with the school."

I fell silent as I thought for a second, then started flipping through the pages of notes again.

"What is it?" Jackson asked.

"Maybe it isn't the university. I know the books were found in the library, but maybe it isn't the library but the books themselves. Maybe it doesn't matter where they were found, just that those versions were found in the library. Remember, we went to all those bookstores, and there were different editions of the books. So maybe the killer was looking for those specific versions, and the easiest place to look was at the university library."

"But *why* would they be looking for those books?" he pressed. "You can find books anywhere. Why these?"

"I don't know. But I want to see if either of the victims had copies of those books or any other books in their homes. Maybe they have their own copies of these books. Or we might find other books that could connect to these. I'm going to go to Warren's apartment and see if the landlord will let me in."

"Well, keep me updated," Jackson said. "I have an appointment I need to get to."

I didn't even take the time to be annoyed. My supposed partner was clearly checked out of this entire thing. I knew why. Even if I didn't want to think he would be so petty. With me at the lead, it seemed like

Jackson was trying to get a point across. That if he wasn't going to be in the lead, he would just step back completely and let me try to do it on my own. He was probably just waiting for me to start struggling and not know what to do next, waiting for the phone call of me desperately asking for his help so he could swoop in and take over.

He wanted to make sure that he was never picked over or put beneath me again. I wasn't going to give him the satisfaction. It didn't matter if I had to do this entire investigation by myself, I was going to get it done. If he was there to take some of it on, fine. If he wasn't, I wasn't going to let that matter.

The landlord was already waiting at the apartment building by the time I walked up to it. The tiny gravel lot set aside for the residents of the building was full, including what the information sheet about Warren Mason told her was his vehicle. That meant I had to participate in the time-honored tradition of finding somewhere to park on the infamously packed Museum District streets. Bordering the historic Fan District—named for the unique shape mapped out for the trolley car system when the area was first established in the early 1800s—this residential area was lively and dynamic but showed its age with the width of the streets.

Parking down here was like a sport—from navigating the often-one-way roads, to finding a patch of space actually big enough to accommodate another vehicle, to finally maneuvering into the coveted spot while trying to avoid completely stopping the flow of traffic for the rest of the street. It could be a bit of a breathless thrill, and I would admit to several times being in cars that erupted in applause and celebration when the task was completed on particularly raucous nights during my college years.

That morning though, I didn't have the luxury of being amused by the process or happy about the spot I finally found. Wanting to make up for the time it took to park, and also just hating the feeling of being watched by somebody standing on a porch as I walked up to them, I broke into a light jog for the last stretch of the sidewalk to the apartment.

"Agent Thorne," I said as I got to the bottom of the steps leading onto the porch, "we spoke on the phone."

"Cyrus Clint," the landlord said with a little inflection and even less emotion. He was already holding the key in his hand and walking over to the door to insert it into the lock. "Cops already searched the place. Did a pretty good number on it too. It's going to take so much time and fucking money to get it back together. Excuse my language."

There was the emotion. This was a man who didn't put a lot of emphasis on interactions with other people but was very sensitive about the way his properties were managed. It didn't so much matter that one of his tenants was brutally murdered. He cared about the condition of the apartment and the work that was going to have to be put into getting it back into rentable condition. Not that he'd be doing it personally, anyway.

I decided to leave the pleasure of letting him know it was going to be a long time before that apartment would be released and to direct any questions to Detective Tarrant.

There were still remnants of the yellow police line stuck to the edges of the doorframe, and a lockbox had been added to the door. The key in Cyrus's hand wasn't the one he would usually use to access the unit. Instead, it was the one for the box that had been put in the apartment for an extra layer of security and to ensure investigators could access it whenever necessary. There was no way to know who might have an extra key to Warren's apartment, and they didn't want to risk someone getting curious about the scene and venturing into it.

The landlord mentioned the police had already searched the apartment, as if he believed such an investigation was a one-and-done type of situation. Like they got one pass through the crime scene and would find everything there was to be found during that one search.

Cyrus walked into the apartment first, stepping out of the way to let me in before closing the door. He stood off to the side nearly pressed against the wall, like he wanted to keep himself as separated as he could from the rest of the space.

Not that I could particularly blame him for that reaction. As unassuming as the old apartment building looked from the outside, inside was complete chaos. The place where Warren's body was found was still clearly visible on the wooden floor, the dark stain of his blood destroying once-beautiful hardwood. There had been some effort to clean up the scene, but a professional crew hadn't yet come in, by the looks of the spatter across one wall and speckling on the beige suede sofa against another. People would like to think if their home became a crime scene, evidence of it would be cleaned up and removed as a basic part of the investigation. This, however, isn't the case. Investigators only collect what is needed and generally leave the rest behind.

This means family, friends, or property owners are responsible for cleaning up what they should never have to see and getting the space back to what it used to be. The rise of professional crime scene cleaning and restoration companies eased this burden, helping people directly affected by horrific situations like this heal and move forward without suffering additional trauma.

I wasn't as much worried about Cyrus being traumatized by what happened in his tenement. But I had absolutely no doubt he was waiting for the instant the apartment was no longer needed for investigation. Then he could call in a team that would clean up and empty it all out so he could replace the floor, repaint the walls, and pretend nothing had ever happened.

"I'm not the police," I made sure to point out to him as I moved further into the room.

"I noticed that," he said. "You said you're a special agent. FBI?"

"Yes," I answered, walking around the perimeter of the living room to observe it from all angles.

I wanted to put myself in the moment of Warren's death, to try to see exactly how it all played out. In the absence of an eyewitness, the crime scene itself must become the witness. Everything from the direction something had fallen when it was knocked over to the type of blood spatter on the walls provides valuable insight into reconstructing the scene. I was trying to visualize that now, hoping to get a feel for exactly how Warren's life came to an end.

"Seems a little quick to already bring in the Feds, doesn't it?" Cyrus asked.

I looked at him for a few silent seconds. He shifted around uncomfortably before I spoke.

"Have you ever been close to a murder like this, Mr. Clint?"

"No."

"Ever seen anything like this?"

"No," he answered, sounding less pleasant with each exchange.

"Then perhaps you leave those judgments up to the people who do this," I said, turning away from him and moving further across the room.

A bookshelf integrated into the wall caught my attention. Collectibles and framed pictures took up most of the room on the shelves, but there were several books. They didn't look as though anyone had so much as picked them up, much less closely examined them. I took out my phone and took pictures to ensure everything was put back exactly as it was, then I made a voice note about the books and my intentions to examine them. That finished, I grabbed as many of the books as I could carry at once and brought them over to an empty dining table. Setting them down, I pulled a chair out and sat. Cyrus let out a heavy sigh when he saw me settle in.

"I thought you were just going to look around. I didn't realize you were going to take a long time. I do have other things I need to do," he said.

"And I have two most likely connected murders to solve," I told him. "You're welcome to leave the key with me. I'll be sure to lock up when I leave."

I really had no need for him to be there while I went through the books. He had already given a thorough statement to the police, who were confident the landlord had nothing to do with the murder and also had no valuable information to offer the investigation. At this point, he was basically just hovering around, making me uneasy. I would much rather be alone.

Cyrus didn't seem to like the idea, but he also didn't want to linger around without any idea of how long this was going to take. He set the key down on the entryway table and left. Alone in the silent apartment, I started the painstaking examination of each of the books. The first pass was comparing the titles to the ones that appeared in the case. When I didn't find any of the same books, I started going through each book, page by page, looking for torn sections or underlined passages.

It took a few hours, but I finally got through all the books and returned them to the shelves. Disappointed at not finding anything in any of the books, I sighed. I had hoped that would have been a jumping-off point, something to connect the apparent clues with the first victim. Now I knew I would have to go back even further and get to know the victims as much as I could to find out who wanted them dead and why.

CHAPTER SEVEN

It was getting late in the day, so I got dinner from one of my favorite takeout spots and brought it back to the apartment. Rather than settling in for a lazy evening, I spread the food out on the coffee table in the living room and opened up my laptop so I could dive into research about Warren Mason.

While there are always exceptions and random victims are certainly prevalent among serial killers, the truth remains that most murder victims are killed by somebody they know. That makes understanding the victim and their life crucial to piecing together a timeline and course of events that eventually culminated in their death.

I delved into investigating Warren Mason thinking that I was going to stumble on something that would point me at least in a starting direction. Maybe he had a police record or a history of conflicts with neighbors or coworkers. Maybe he owned a business and recently fired workers and they were angered by the situation.

Instead, there was nothing. I learned he wasn't from the Richmond area but had moved there several years before. This was the second apartment he'd lived in, and there was nothing negative about the move, just that the lease ended and he decided to try something else. There were no records of anything beyond some traffic violations and a single report of being drunk in public the year before. He'd never spent any time in jail or been accused of any violence. He worked in a medical records office supplying information to fill subpoenas, liked to rock climb and go whitewater rafting on weekends, and overall seemed to live a very normal life. I couldn't find any indication of conflict or bad blood that might have made him a target.

With Warren Mason feeling like a dead end at least for the moment, I moved on to research Danielle Scherer. This young woman was a fairly stark contrast to Warren. In her early twenties, she was already in graduate school and had plans for another degree after completing the one she was studying. She was active in the writing club as well as several organizations on campus. Just a quick glance through her public social media showed that she had what seemed like an enviable life, including a long-term relationship with a boyfriend everyone considered incredibly sweet and a fantastic catch.

Danielle was very well liked and respected among fellow students and faculty alike. It didn't seem like she was into the party scene at all, but rather was studious, creative, and sensitive. When her posts weren't about her boyfriend or what she was doing with her student organizations at any given time, they were beautiful images accompanied by thoughtful captions that showed a girl with a deep connection to the world around her and an appreciation for life.

Noticing there wasn't any contact information for her family listed in the case files, I sent messages to the family members listed among her social media contacts as well as her boyfriend. It was too late to attempt any other communication, and I wanted to get an early start, so I headed to bed with a set alarm and hoped the next day would bring more answers.

Waking up early, I checked the phone for responses to the social media messages before even getting out of bed. There was nothing. A couple were marked as read, but they'd been ignored, and the others still hadn't been seen. I got up and spent my customary hour on the stationary bike sitting in the corner of my room then got into the shower. As I was tossing everything I could get my hands on into the blender for a breakfast smoothie, my phone dinged.

It was from Nathan Garrett, Danielle's boyfriend. The message sounded cautious, but he said he was willing to meet up with me and talk about Danielle. I checked again and saw that now all the messages to Danielle's family had been seen, but there were still no responses from anyone. Deciding I couldn't wait around to hear from them, I decided to take advantage of the opportunity to speak with Nathan.

The young man was sitting on the stone steps of a small amphitheater near the library and dining hall at the center of campus when I found him. Curled in on himself with his arms tucked tight between his chest and thighs, he looked like he was trying to disappear as much as he was warding off the cold of the stiff wind that had picked up. The sky was a soft gray, almost white, threatening snow that hadn't come for the holidays but might decide to interfere and cause trouble now.

"Nathan?"

He looked up, and I offered what I hoped was at least a somewhat comforting smile.

"Agent Thorne," he said.

"You can call me Callan," I said. I gestured behind me toward the student commons building. "Want to go in and grab something hot to drink? Or we could go somewhere else."

"Sure," he said. "There's a place not too far from here."

It made sense that he was avoiding the commons. He was without a doubt experiencing tremendous emotional turmoil, and it was unlikely he was in the kind of mental space to handle being surrounded by other students. As popular as Danielle was, and as well-known as they were as a couple, he would be the center of attention. The thought of that made his folded-over position and hat pulled down close to his eyes even more understandable. It helped conceal his face so he could have some time to himself rather than grapple with people wanting to mine him for details or suffocate him with what they thought was reassurance and support.

"Is it within walking distance, or do you want a ride?" I asked.

But just as the words were out of my mouth, a harsh wind whipped around us, and he shivered. That was enough of an answer. We walked to my car, and I followed Nathan's directions back toward the Fan District.

I somehow managed to find a parking spot close to the tiny corner coffee shop he pointed out.

"This was Danielle's favorite place to get breakfast or a snack," he told me, his voice powdery with emotion. "Her apartment is just a couple of blocks from here."

I climbed out of the car. "Danielle lived near here?"

"Yeah, you can actually see her building." Nathan stood beside me and pointed, leaning slightly like he was trying to get a better look. "That brick one with all the blue-and-purple stuff all over the balcony. Her Christmas decorations are still up. That's actually the back of the complex. You have to go into it from the other side."

I looked at the apartment and then glanced around. We were only about four streets away from Warren's apartment. I didn't know if that was significant, considering this was a densely populated area of the city, but I took note to keep it in mind.

We went into the coffee shop. I remembered it being a laundromat when I was in school. A friend of mine lived across the street. Every time I walked in there, there was a strange feeling of knowing I was standing right at the place where my friend and I once ended up taking over all the machines at the same time in order to get all our laundry done because we hadn't done it for a couple of weeks. The ceiling was still covered with the original copper tiles put there in the 1920s before it was a laundromat, and the cracked tile floor had just been pieced back together and sealed rather than replaced. I knew for a fact one of those cracks was specifically my fault.

We ordered and brought our drinks and pastries out to the patio built up from the foundation of what used to be a small house beside the building. A wood-framed gazebo offered a heated respite from the cold while still providing the privacy I wanted Nathan to have for what I knew was going to be a difficult and painful conversation.

He sipped his Black Eye, a high-octane combination of black coffee with a double shot of espresso poured directly into the middle to create the visual, but only stared at the ham-and-cheese pastry he'd chosen. I savored several sips of herbal tea heavily augmented with honey, giving Nathan time to adjust before starting. I tore a piece of puff pastry away from my mushroom-and-onion tart, and as I was putting it in my mouth, he lifted wide brown eyes to me.

"Who would have done something like this to Danielle?" he asked.

"I was hoping you would be able to help me answer that," I told him. "I didn't know her. I know you did. Very well."

Nathan nodded. "Yeah, I did. Really well. For years. I don't know what I'm going to do without her."

The words cut into me, but I didn't let it show.

"I'm so sorry for your loss. I know you're going through something unimaginably hard right now, and the last thing you want to do is talk about it."

"I already talked to the police about it. And I've talked to everybody who can get anywhere near me about it. After I talked to you about meeting up, I turned off my phone so I could get a little bit of peace," Nathan said.

"I'm sorry I'm asking you to go through it all again. But I'm just starting my investigation, and I need as much information as I can possibly get. The better I can know Danielle and what was going on in her life, the better chance I have of getting to the person who did this to her and stopping them from doing it to somebody else," I said.

Nathan took a longer sip of the coffee that had been cooled by the air outside. He stared at his hand wrapped around the cup for a moment then swallowed hard.

"What do you want to know?"

An hour later, I was driving back to campus feeling like I knew Danielle better but like I was still in the same place where I started. Nathan was able to confirm that she was adored by the people who knew her but that she kept her true inner circle close. She wasn't the kind of person to go out partying and preferred to be at home or spend time with him and maybe one or two of their closest friends. She was passionate about the things she cared about and was looking ahead to a successful, happy future. He never would have thought something like this could happen to her. She didn't have any enemies. She'd never hurt anyone. In his opinion, it had to be random.

Somehow that made it worse.

After dropping Nathan off, I decided to speak with some of her professors to find out what they could tell me about the promising young woman who had been taken from them far too soon. While talking with friends, family members, and romantic partners was obviously important to understanding a murder victim and what, if anything, in their lives could have put them in the path of their killer, it was also critical to go beyond those more intimate connections to the people who interacted with them on a different level. For a dedicated student and high-achieving member of the campus culture, that meant exploring her engagement with the faculty and those involved with the organizations.

I drove to the other side of campus and parked, intending to go to the humanities building first. Everything that I'd found out about Danielle pointed to a great passion for writing, so I wanted to talk to the faculty adviser of the creative writing club first. I was still a few blocks from the building when I noticed something going on outside.

Quickening my steps, I made my way down to the thick crowd gathered in the courtyard in front of the humanities building and spilling out onto the sidewalk. The students were shouting, some holding up signs, many recording the whole chaotic scene on their phones. It was a demonstration, but I couldn't figure out what they were protesting. The shouts were overlapping and blending so much it was almost impossible to hear what any of them were saying.

"Killer!"

That one word punctuated the overall rush of sound, and I whipped around to try to find who had shouted it. An angry-looking young man behind me locked eyes with me. I noticed he was holding a poster board with a picture of a woman at the center and names of authors and books scribbled around it.

Without any other context, it wasn't a very effective sign, but he was gripping it with an intensity that spoke to just how passionately he believed in whatever he was screaming about.

"Get her off campus!" someone else shouted.

"Why is she still here?" yelled another.

"What's going on?" I asked loudly, leaning toward the man.

"There she is!"

The crowd suddenly rushed forward. I got swept into the motion, my body tumbled and pushed as the group seemed to move as one unit toward the building. They were still shouting, and I felt the heated energy building. This could get violent very quickly. I grabbed the badge hanging around my neck and pulled it out from under my coat. Shoving it toward the man, I made sure he saw it.

"What the hell is going on?" I repeated.

He pushed out of the crowd, and I followed.

"You're a cop?" asked the guy, who I guessed at five or so years younger than me, likely a graduate student.

"FBI," I told him. "What is this about?"

"Professor Campano."

I knew the name. It was exactly who I was there to see.

"The faculty adviser of the creative writing club?" she asked.

"Yeah. The blood in the books? The quotes? She has ones like that posted all over her classroom. Anytime you talk to that woman, she has a quote from some book she thinks has to do with what's going on. Everybody knew she was jealous of Danielle. Now the school is letting a murderer keep teaching."

CHAPTER EIGHT

"Get them away from here," I demanded.

"We have the right to free speech and peaceful demonstration."

"There's nothing peaceful about a mob going after a woman. You're blocking people from getting to class and causing a dangerous situation. Stop this shit, and get them away," I said.

Forcing my way through the crowd with my badge held high and visible, I made my way to the door to the building. Two men were standing in front, their own tags around their necks identifying them as faculty from the building.

"You're not coming in here," one of them shouted. "You need to get away from here."

"She needs to get off this campus," one of the protestors shouted. "You're harboring a murderer."

"We've called the police," the other said.

I got to the door and showed them my badge. "Special Agent Callan Thorne. I'm with the FBI. I need to speak with Professor Campano."

The men moved out of the way enough to let me through the door. As it closed behind me, I could hear the sirens in the distance as police approached. The crowd quickly dissipated with only a handful of the most-ardent demonstrators standing their ground, facing the men defending the door. I had already looked up the room number for the professor's office, so I ran up the steps toward the third floor.

When I reached the office, I noticed remnants of torn paper clinging to the outside of the door and a piece of cloth put over the narrow window set in the center. I knocked on the door.

A hesitant voice responded, "Yes?"

"Professor Campano, this is Agent Callan Thorne. I'm with the FBI. Can I have a moment to speak with you?" I asked.

There was the sound of a lock disengaging, and the door opened slightly. The woman from the poster looked out at me from the narrow space between the door and the frame. I showed her my badge and waited for the professor to examine it then opened the door the rest of the way.

"Come in," she said. "Shut the door."

"Thank you." I walked in and shut the door behind me, staying close to it in case there was a need to react. "Are you all right?"

Professor Campano paced back and forth in the small office like she couldn't stand still. Her thick, sandy-brown hair had been twisted up into a bun on the back of her head and secured in place with a clip, but several pieces had fallen out in her rush from the crowd. She wore a cream sweater with a camel-colored skirt that came down over brown leather boots. A long wool coat, the same color as the skirt, had been tossed over the back of one of the chairs in the room. She looked so effortlessly put together and yet so shaken up at the same time.

She looked at me and shook her head.

"I don't even know how to answer that. I was just trying to get to work. I have classes to teach and a writing club to facilitate. I thought that the hardest thing that was going to happen today was going to that club and helping the students work through what everybody was feeling after Danielle's death. I had no idea I was going to be facing all this."

"I can't imagine that was easy," I said.

Professor Campano scoffed and shook her head, then paused and looked at me, her eyes narrowing questioningly.

"Who did you say you are?" she asked. "Did you say FBI?"

"Yes. Special Agent Callan Thorne. Please call me Callan."

"Stephanie Campano. You can call me Stephanie. Are you here because of Danielle?" she asked.

"I am. Richmond PD reached out to the Bureau and asked us to get involved after Danielle's body was found. There are only two victims, but the methods are showing the hallmarks of a potential serial killer, and that's not something to be taken lightly, especially when it involves students. I've taken the lead on the investigation," I said. "I actually came here to talk to you about Danielle. I wasn't expecting to run into the mob downstairs either. Can you explain to me what they are so worked up about? One of them said something about quotes?"

Stephanie rolled her eyes and swept her hands back from her forehead to smooth the loose hair back into place. "This is so ridiculous."

Before she could say anything else, another knock on her door stopped her. Her eyes widened as she looked at the door. I stepped in front of her.

"Yes?" I called out.

There was a slight pause. "Stephanie?"

"This is Special Agent Callan Thorne," I replied.

"Is Stephanie there? It's Miranda."

I looked back at Stephanie, who nodded.

"She's another professor," she explained. "You can let her in."

I opened the door and let the woman on the other side stick her head into the office. She was a decade or so older than Stephanie and wore her dark, curly hair to her shoulders. Big blue eyes searched Professor Campano with concern.

"Are you okay? I just heard about what's going on," she said.

"I'm fine," Stephanie said. "Just shaken up and, you know, honestly a bit pissed off. These tragedies happened right here, and yet instead of pulling together to try to show support and help each other through something this horrible, they're acting like they want to take up pitchforks and torches. They'd rather be down there hurling accusations than actually comforting each other or trying to be helpful in finding out what really happened."

"Are you going to cancel your classes for the afternoon?" Miranda asked.

Stephanie crossed her arms over her chest. "Absolutely not. I'm not going to get run off campus by them. I'm here to teach, and that's exactly what I'm going to do… if there are any students to come to the class or if they are allowed inside."

"The police were nearly here when I was coming inside. I'm sure they've gotten it under control by this point. When does your class start?" I asked.

Stephanie glanced at the time. "Fifteen minutes. I really need to get to the room."

"Let me come with you," I said.

Despite her assertion that she wasn't going to allow the students to force her off campus, Stephanie looked upset and scared. Her arms tightened around her, and she nodded.

"Good," Miranda said. "You shouldn't be walking around here alone. I was going to walk with you one way or another, but this one looks like she can keep things under control."

Stephanie grabbed a satchel and a stack of books along with a coffee cup, and we headed out of the office. She locked the door behind us, and I noticed her eyes flicker over the ripped paper clinging to the door.

"What happened there?" I asked.

"When I got up here, there were some papers on the door. They weren't exactly notes of encouragement and commendation." She let out a mirthless chuckle. "It will never cease to amaze me how fast people can go from commendation to condemnation, you know?"

I couldn't place that as being from anything specifically, but it felt like the kind of inspirational quote that would show up on a coffee tumbler or a sign in front of a church leading up to a revival. Which I had never personally attended, but I figured it was something along the lines of a church sweeps week.

"Where's the classroom?" I asked, stepping in front of the other two.

I didn't want to say I was going to walk in front of them on the off chance that some of the protestors had made their way inside the building and the professor could be at risk. She felt safe now that she'd gotten into the building, and I didn't want to compromise that. But I was very aware of the possibility of something else happening. Even with the police breaking up the demonstration and sending the students on their way, she was still at risk. The group was whipped into a frenzy by something, and so far I hadn't been able to find the kind of significance in it that would justify that reaction.

Rather than the lack of foundation beneath their anger making me feel any better about the whole thing, it actually made me feel more wary. Mob mentality is a very real thing. People who generally think clearly and behave like normal people can get completely swept up by the pulsating energy of a crowd, emboldened by the people around them. With their inhibitions taken from them, they could do things they would never do without the escalation of the mob. And that can have extremely dangerous consequences.

The fact that they had such an intense reaction meant they were already volatile. Being confronted and challenged by the men at the doors, by me, and by the police who came to break up the demonstration—not to mention Stephanie Campano herself forcing through them to get inside despite their efforts—would only make them more aggressive.

The protestors believed they were in the right. They saw the efforts against them as oppression and injustice, which would make them think of getting to the professor a coup. She wasn't yet safe. Not until there was time for this whole situation to cool off and everyone to calm down. I had a sinking feeling that wasn't going to be as easy as just waiting for some time to pass.

They pointed out the location of the classroom, and I led them to it. Students waiting inside looked relieved when Stephanie walked into the room. One young man hopped down from the desk where he was sitting and came toward her.

"Are you okay? We heard something was happening outside," he said.

"You heard?" I asked. "You didn't see anyone out there?"

I doubted all signs of the group and the police interaction would be gone in the time it would take for me to get to the office and then back here. He looked at me with a questioning expression, and I saw his eyes flicker down to the badge visible over my shirt.

"I was already in class upstairs," he told me. "I didn't leave the building."

"This is Agent Thorne," Stephanie said. "She's investigating… what happened."

"We're still having our meeting later, right?" a girl asked from her seat.

"Of course, we are. Like I told Agent Thorne, I'm not letting them force me away from my job. I did nothing wrong. They aren't going to intimidate me."

I glanced around the room as she moved over toward the desk in the front corner of the room to put down her coat and papers.

"Do you always have your meetings in this room?" I asked.

Stephanie nodded. "Yeah. Almost all of my classes and my creative writing club meetings are held here."

Signs hung around the walls plastered the room with the quotes the students outside had been talking about. Some were simple pieces of poster board with the words written in a thick marker. Others had been printed out on a computer. Still others looked like purchased posters, like the ones I remembered from my elementary school book fair days. But it still seemed like a pretty big stretch to me. I couldn't recall a single English teacher I'd ever had class with, from elementary school to college, that didn't have quotes on their wall. What made Stephanie's room more unique, though, was that many of these pieces were obviously handcrafted or custom-designed, and the room was practically bursting in them.

I pointed out a particularly complex cross-stitched picture featuring a quote from Shakespeare in lettering that resembled the illuminated manuscripts of the time.

"Do you have quotes like these around all the time?" I asked.

"Yes. I have them up here in my classroom. I have a couple in my office you might not have noticed. I put them on my syllabi. If I am communicating with the class, I use one after my signature on an email. It's something I've done since before I was even in college. I'm passionate about the written word. As cliché and ridiculous as that might sound. But I would think that would be fairly obvious, considering my career path. I am sure I'm not the only English professor in the world who has famous quotes from great works of literature around them."

"I'm sure you're right," I said. "But those professors aren't teaching on a campus where quotes are linked to two murders."

"Are you saying you think she had something to do with it?" the guy asked, his voice edging on aggression.

"Anthony, calm down. Agent Thorne is here to help. She isn't accusing me of anything." Stephanie's eyes slid over to me. "Right?"

"I'm not accusing you," I said. "I'm pointing out the reasons people might be on edge. You're right—other teachers do this as well. But clearly whatever whipped this mob up focused on that—and you—immediately. They were trying to keep you out of class, your club meeting, and off campus because when they heard about the passages from the books, the first person they thought of was you."

"I'm worried they are just going to keep coming after you," the girl said, her eyes wide, a sheer veil of tears glazing over them.

Stephanie walked over to the girl and rubbed her back, looking at me again. "This is Kaylee. She and Anthony are both in the creative writing club."

"Stephanie?"

A man's voice in the hallway made us all turn, and a second later, a tall man wearing the kind of thick, black glasses that could be either very trendy or very outdated walked past, then turned back and came into the room. His frame was almost skeletal, his arms and legs so long they looked like he could easily lose control of their movements.

"Hey, Asher," Stephanie said, holding up her hands. "It's all right. I'm fine."

"That's not what I heard." He looked at me, and his face clouded over slightly. It was like he was recognizing a stranger in the midst and didn't like the intrusion.

"Agent Callan Thorne," I said, extending my hand to shake his. "I'm with the FBI. I'm here to investigate the situation happening on campus."

"The situation?" he asked. "Are you talking about the murders?"

Kaylee flinched, and I noticed Anthony take a subtle step toward her at the same time Miranda and Stephanie stepped closer as well. They were physically closing ranks, even if they didn't consciously realize they were doing it.

"Local police asked the Bureau to intervene, and I was put as lead in the case," I tell him.

"At least it's good to hear they are taking this seriously. I'm glad they didn't hesitate to ask for more assistance. I'm Asher Vance. I teach psychology."

At that moment, a younger man looking nearly the same age as the students came into the room carrying an armful of folders and papers.

"And ever the master of timing, this is my assistant, Marcus."

"I thought you'd be in your office," Marcus said.

"I'm sorry. I needed to come see Professor Campano. Did everybody get their papers turned in?" Asher asked.

"Looks like it. A couple of them don't look long enough, but I don't think anybody's missing."

"Ridiculous. They think I'm not going to notice them not meeting the requirements of the assignment because they at least turned it in. I wish I knew why mediocrity became acceptable," Asher grumbled.

I suddenly felt like it was nine years ago and I was sitting in my own psychology class hoping the hardline professor would be impressed by the insights in my term paper. Maybe it was just something about professors in that discipline.

"And on that note, I think we should go ahead and get started with class. I don't know if anyone else is going to come or it's just the small crowd today."

"We should get started on grading those," Asher said, nodding toward the papers in Marcus's arms. "Stephanie, are you sure you're all right?"

"I'm fine. Thank you," Stephanie said.

"Wait, I don't think we should both leave," Miranda said. "She should have someone with her. I have to go teach a class, but, Asher, aren't you done for the day?"

"No, seriously, you don't have to do this," Stephanie protested, waving her hands in front of them. "It's fine."

"It's not fine, Stephanie," Miranda said. "And you know it isn't."

"She's right," Asher said. "I didn't see what was going on out there, but from what I heard, it got pretty intense. You really should take precautions. At least for a little while. I finished teaching for the day. I just need to do this grading, and I'm supposed to meet with a student later. I can just do the grading here. Marcus and I can sit in the corner. You won't even know we're here."

"You're not going to be able to focus with us having our discussion over here," Stephanie said.

"If I can't, I'll let you know and go back to my office. But I'm sure it'll be fine," Asher said. "Remember, I did grow up with very loud twin brothers and a small herd of dogs. I've learned to filter out distractions."

Stephanie nodded as if she'd heard that before and gestured for him to go to the back of the room.

"Can any of you tell me anything about the murders? Your initial impressions, thoughts, anything?" I asked the students.

"We didn't come here to be interrogated," one of the students said.

"I'm not interrogating you. I'm asking for some insight. This is my job, but I also went to school here, so I'm protective of the campus and everyone on it. I'd assume you would feel the same way. But you also know the people involved. At least Danielle," I said.

"Again, she's here to help," Stephanie said. "She's not one of the people down there in the mob. You don't need to be so defensive."

"The library doesn't have surveillance," Kaylee said. "Not inside anyway. There are a couple of cameras outside."

"But they face away from the building," Anthony says. "They cover the campus at the center of the buildings and the walkways."

"That is in the report from the police. That they didn't have any footage of the person bringing the books in or putting them on the shelves or anything. So identifying who did this isn't going to be as easy as just finding footage of them tearing the books or putting the blood in them," I said.

"You think it was done in the library?" Stephanie asked. "They didn't bring those books in already like that?"

"I can't really answer that," I said.

"The library is almost always busy. But it's not exactly a place that people go to socialize. If you're in there, you're studying or looking for a book. Not exactly paying attention to what's going on around you. Even if someone interacted with this person or was even right there while they were doing it, they probably didn't notice. I know I'm so focused on what I'm doing when I'm in there that I wouldn't be able to tell you who was there or what was happening," Anthony said.

"But the question is, did this person know that and that's why they did it that way, or is it just a convenient coincidence for them?" Asher asked.

"Are we going to talk about it in crime club today?" Anthony asked.

Asher shifted his weight, his eyes flickering back and forth between Stephanie and Anthony then me, like he wished he hadn't said anything and was uncomfortable being put on the spot.

"I'd considered it," he admitted. "It seemed like something everyone might be interested in. But now that all this is happening, maybe it isn't appropriate."

"Crime club?" I asked. "What's that?"

"It isn't really a club," Asher said. "It's just what the students call my Psychology of Crime class. Basically, it's an advanced-level class that combines psychology and criminology to prepare students interested in a future career in law enforcement, forensics, criminal psychology, or even the legal field for things they might face in their future careers. We study famous cases through the lens of psychology and techniques such as profiling and forensic evaluation."

As elaborate as his description of the class sounded, it was a fairly straightforward, basic course offered in many universities. In fact, I took one like it when I was going to school there. It was one of my favorite classes. This sounded like a much more involved version but with the same basic intention.

"What do you mean inappropriate?" Anthony asked. "Isn't this kind of thing the whole point of the class?"

"The point of the class is to help students understand the human mind better and use those skills to better understand crime, criminals, and how to solve crimes when they do happen or reduce the risk that they will happen in the first place," Asher said. "This is a very real situation. And the effect it is having on the people on campus is serious. They put Professor Campano in physical danger this morning. They are so worked up, and something like the class discussing the details of the cases could just push them even further."

"So we stop doing something that could be important because some people are going crazy?" Anthony asked.

"I agree with Professor Vance," I said. "I really do understand that desire to talk about this and try to get to the bottom of it, but it's also important to balance that with not making the situation worse. I'm here to investigate. That's my job, and I will take it step by step the way it needs to be handled."

A few other students filtered into the room, and I took that as my cue to leave.

"I'll be around, so you can contact me whenever if you think of anything that might be important. Let me know if anything else threatening happens."

Stephanie nodded, and I said goodbye to the rest of the group before walking out of the room. Jackson was calling as I left the building.

"Thorne," I said, glancing around to see if I could catch sight of any lingering protesters who hadn't been fully dispersed by the police.

"Checking in," Jackson said.

"Good. Meet me at the university library."

"Be there in ten," he said.

I waited just inside the door for Jackson to arrive. He shuffled toward the building with his hands shoved deep in his pockets and his head tucked down low against the cold. We walked over to a corner where we were out of earshot.

"The library needs to be under surveillance. There's very little in the way of security or surveillance here already. No cameras inside. And the only ones that are outside aren't really focused on the entrances and exits of the building," I said.

"You think we should wait until somebody else is murdered?" Jackson asked.

"That's not what I said. I said the library needs to be under surveillance. This killer is acting in a sequence. The torn page is the first warning of a death coming. Remember, the book with the torn section was turned in to the librarians by that student before the book was found with the blood. It had to be done first, because of the age of the blood and the fact that that book had been returned to the library after the torn one. It wouldn't have been available to have that passage underlined before. If we're going to operate under the theory that this is a serial killer, another murder could be planned. Watching at the library and monitoring every book that comes in as well as searching the current books on the stacks can give a warning and stop that from happening."

He gave me a look. "Whatever you say."

CHAPTER NINE

I CHOSE ONE OF THE QUIET STUDY ROOMS TOWARD THE BACK OF THE library for my home base of the investigation. The librarians provided me with a key so I could lock up my materials when I wasn't there, but with the library still active, I was reluctant to leave anything sensitive behind. It took the rest of the day and the next to manage the logistics of securing the library and putting it under surveillance while also still permitting students and faculty to use it without hindrance. I didn't want people to know the library was being watched.

I wanted to streamline the process of reviewing every book as it was returned and do it out of view of anyone not directly connected to the plan. That included the student volunteers and workers getting financial aid hours or academic experience by working at the library. Only the primary librarians and staff knew what was going on, and I emphasized several times the critical importance of them not revealing this information to anybody else.

With the surveillance and book review process put into place, we started the long and time-consuming effort of going through every single page of the books in the stacks. Not only did I want to make sure that there was a basic understanding of the condition of every book so it could be effectively and appropriately compared if that book was checked out of the library and then returned, but I also wanted to make sure no warnings had been missed.

Halfway through the second day going over the books, I got a message from Detective Tarrant letting me know that Warren Mason's next of kin was finally able to come to the city and claim his belongings. It was our last chance to go through the apartment as it was when he was killed. I thanked her for telling me and sought out Jackson going through books in another corner of the library.

"Come on," I told him. "We're going to Warren Mason's apartment. It's going to be emptied out, and this is one more opportunity for us to look over it and get any insight or evidence we can."

Jackson looked hesitant, his eyes flickering back to the box like he didn't want to leave the task he was already on, but there were several others assisting with the process, so I insisted he come along. Because it was the middle of the day and most people living in the neighborhood were either at school or work, it was easier to find a parking spot. Ready with the key the landlord gave me, I hurried up the sidewalk to the building. As we approached, I saw a woman standing on the porch, her back to us as she seemed to look up and down the street like she was waiting for someone.

"Hello?" I called.

The woman turned around, and I saw surprise flicker across her face. I walked up to her with my hand extended, making sure my badge was visible on my chest.

"Hi. I'm Special Agent Callan Thorne, from the FBI," I said.

"Mallory Mason," she said, her eyes moving over my shoulder and then back to me. "Warren is my brother."

"I'm so sorry for your loss. I am investigating what happened and can assure you everything is being done to find out who is responsible for Warren's death."

"Thank you," she said.

I stepped slightly to the side and gestured at Jackson. "This is my partner…"

"Jackson?" she said, sounding both shocked and unsure of what she was saying. "Jackson Blanchard?"

My stomach sank a little, and I turned to look at Jackson. His jaw was hard, his hands shoved in his pockets again. His eyes weren't showing any kind of surprise the way hers was.

"Hey, Mallory," he said. "It's been a long time."

Mallory hurried down the porch steps and ran a few feet to Jackson, throwing her arms around him in a tight hug.

"I'm so glad you're here. I had no idea you were working on this case. I wish somebody had told me," she said. "It makes me feel so much better to know you're a part of this. Warren would have wanted it that way."

"You two know each other?" I asked.

Jackson took Mallory by the hips and subtly pulled her away from him. He set her to the side, and she nodded at me, wiping tears from under her eyes.

"Yes. It's been a long time. How many years, Jackson?"

"I don't know," he said, his voice low and monotone. He was clearly not as enthralled by this reunion as Mallory evidently was.

"A lot," she said. "More than ten, I know that. I'm sure he's told you all about Warren. I guess it makes sense he wouldn't mention me, well, with everything going on. But I'm just really happy to see him." She looked at Jackson again. "I really am. I'm so happy to see you. I know things weren't great, but he really would want you to be a part of this. It would mean the world to him. I don't even know if he knew you were in town."

"I don't think he did," Jackson said. "I didn't know he was here either."

"But you still ended up in the investigation. Just the way it should be," she said.

He looked at me, his eyes meeting mine with a heavy, dark expression. I didn't show the confusion and anger I was feeling. That was a conversation for later when she wasn't around. For now I needed this last opportunity to go through the apartment, and now that I'd met Warren's sister, I wanted to talk with her about her brother. Even if she had no idea who did this to him or why, she knew him. Just being able to learn more about him as a person and the life he had led before his murder could really help me round out my view of him and how he could have ended up as one of the victims.

Despite my focus and concentration on going through the apartment one last time and talking with Mallory about Warren, I was still angry when I finished my conversation with her and left her to the task of packing up the apartment. She assured me there were some other people coming by to help and there wasn't much in the small apartment anyway, so she could handle it. I left her with my contact information, and we got back in the car.

Immediately, I turned to Jackson.

"What the hell is that all about?" I asked. "Why was the sister of the victim of a murder you are supposed to be investigating cozying up to you and talking about your relationship with that victim like you were best friends?"

"We weren't best friends. But we were close," he said.

I scoffed incredulously. "Oh wow, that makes all the difference in the world. It would be weird and shady as hell if you were best friends with the victim, but if you were just good friends, then it's perfectly okay."

"I know this seems bad," Jackson said. "And I should have said something."

"You're damn right you should have said something," I said. "I stood there looking like an absolute idiot while she babbled on about some mystical connection and how deep your relationship went."

"She didn't say anything about a mystical connection," he said with a heavy sigh.

"Are you seriously going to split hairs about this? That's going to be your defense?' I asked.

"Look, I didn't ask to be a part of this case. Agent Martinez assigned me. I found out that Warren was one of the victims, and it was a shock. We went to school together years ago. In another life, it feels like. A different state. A different era. And yes, we were good friends at that time. We spent a lot of time together, and I got to know his sister really well. Their parents died when they were young, and the two of them were raised by an aunt who was pretty much out of the picture by the time they started college. We were friends through college and then had a falling out. We haven't been in contact in over a decade. It didn't feel relevant," Jackson said.

"It didn't feel relevant? It didn't occur to you that having a personal relationship with the victim, even years ago, was something you should have mentioned to me when investigating a murder?" I asked, stunned by what he was saying.

I couldn't wrap my head around his omission. It was so glaringly obvious that he should have revealed his personal connection to one of the victims. Even just something as simple as having known him in the past or having had any kind of knowledge of him beyond the investigation mattered. It felt deceitful and underhanded. I was already struggling to find a connection with Jackson, and now I felt like he had purposely deceived me and potentially compromised the entire investigation.

"If I thought anything about our friendship could be relevant to this investigation, I would have said something," Jackson said. "But it was more than ten years ago, and we haven't spoken. There wasn't anything huge and dramatic about the end of our friendship. We just kind of started going down different paths and then had a fight and didn't get around to patching it back together before school ended. It really wasn't that big of a deal.

"Mallory is fragile right now. Warren was basically all she had, and losing him had to have been a really serious blow. She is overexaggerating how much of a connection we really had. I can probably pinpoint five or six times in my entire friendship with Warren when I spent any time with Mallory other than just a quick greeting in passing. She's clinging to me because I'm something familiar. It makes her feel better to think that someone other than a stranger is looking into her brother's murder. If something like this happened to you, wouldn't you feel better thinking someone who cared was part of the investigation?" he asked.

My stomach twisted, and I did my best to cover up my hard swallow. I used starting the car and pulling out of the parking spot as an excuse to look away. I wasn't going to answer that.

"Is there anything else you haven't told me? You're sure you didn't have any contact with him at all after you left school? You haven't talked to him? Or run into him?" I asked.

"No. Like I told Mallory, I didn't even know he was here. I was born and raised in Ashland. Being in Richmond was essentially just coming back home for me. I don't know why Warren would come here. He wasn't from here. He was originally from Pennsylvania, if I'm remembering correctly. He never talked about wanting to move here and never got in touch with me to tell me he was. That was part of why it was such a shock to find out he'd been murdered after living here for years," Jackson told me.

It was plausible. For those of us who lived here, Richmond could feel fairly small. I had to remind myself even feeling like that. I didn't know everyone who lived here, and thinking back to my own college experience a decade before, I didn't know what came of the vast majority of the people I interacted with, even those I considered my good friends at the time.

It still felt like a major oversight for him to just not tell me, but I was going to try not to dwell on it for right then. There were too many other things to think about to waste too much time and energy on a distant connection.

After getting something to eat, I headed back toward the library to continue with the search. Jackson had his face buried in his phone as we walked into the building and barely acknowledged me as we parted ways to return to our areas of the stacks. I was watching him, the gears in my brain churning a bit, as I took a few steps in the other direction and nearly ran right into someone coming the other way. I turned just in time and managed to stop, reaching out to grab on to their arms to keep us from colliding.

We stepped apart, and I realized it was one of the students I'd met in Stephanie's classroom the day of the protest.

"I'm sorry," I said. "I wasn't paying attention."

She shook her head. "It's fine. I'm sure you've got a lot going on in your head right now. Agent Thorne, right?"

"Yeah," I said.

"I'm Sydney. I didn't introduce myself the other day," she said.

Some of the hardened attitude was gone, like the time between the confrontation in the classroom and now had softened the edges. But I could still see the tightness in the way she carried herself and the distrust when she looked at me. It was the kind of wariness that came not because she thought I was going to do something to make the situation worse, but more that I was an outsider brought in to handle this and she didn't like that I was coming so close to something that hurt her. I knew that feeling. A long time ago, I had that feeling. In the quiet moments when I was by myself and forced myself to be truly honest, I knew in so many ways I still did.

"How are you dealing with everything?" I asked.

"Scared. Angry. But the group is making it easier. I don't feel so much like I'm just sitting off on the sidelines not doing anything and just waiting for something else to happen," she said.

I tilted my head to the side slightly. "Group? Is the school providing therapy?"

"No. Vance's class. We started discussing the case and are doing a little investigation of it. I know it isn't the same thing that you're doing, but it makes me feel like I'm actually trying to do something about this. Even if we're just trying to better understand why it's happening, that's better than just sitting around and acting like nothing is going wrong. Right?"

"I didn't know that was actually happening. I thought he said it was inappropriate and wasn't going to do it," I said.

Sydney shrugged. "I guess he changed his mind. I've got to get going. I'm already late for math."

"When's the next one of Vance's classes?"

"Six," she said.

"Tonight?" I asked.

"Yeah. Room 348 in the Humanities building."

I nodded and returned her wave as she headed for the door. I was seriously uncomfortable with the sudden change. I thought Asher and I were on the same page when it came to discussing the case or getting the kids wrapped up in trying to be involved.

It was still early in the afternoon, so there was plenty of time for me to continue the search in the library before sitting in on the class. I wanted to know how the class was being handled and what exactly was going on.

I spent the rest of the afternoon split between going over the notes of the case again and searching the books in the stacks. When the time got close, I sought out Jackson and told him about the class.

"I'm heading there now," I said. "I want to know what's being said and talk to the professor about stopping it."

"I can't go with you," Jackson told me. "I've already stayed here longer than I planned to. I've got to go."

I stared at him incredulously. "What are you doing that's more important than solving this?"

"Callan, I've done my job. I've been here all day looking through these books, or up at that apartment trying to find a shred of anything that would give us these answers. We haven't found anything. And I'm not going to stop my life to go sit in a lecture hall and listen to a bunch of college kids try to piece together a crime that FBI agents haven't been able to solve."

"It's been less than a week," I pointed out. "Complicated cases aren't solved that quickly."

"You're the lead investigator on this case. Do what you think you need to do," he said.

He stuffed the book in his hands back on the shelf, scooped his bag and water bottle off the floor, and walked past me. I was pissed but didn't have time to dwell on it. If he was going to skim the surface and do only the bare minimum in this case, so be it. It would get him out of my way and let me do, as he said, what I needed to do.

Thoughts of Jackson's former friendship with Warren Mason flickered through my head, and I tried to feel some compassion. Even if it had been a long time since they were actually friends, his murder would still be an emotional blow. I told myself Jackon's reluctance to get too close or too involved with the case was a matter of it being too painful for him.

But I struggled to make myself believe that. If anything, I would think the connection would make it more important for him to be as involved as possible in the case. He should feel like it was his responsibility, that he, by merit of the friendship they had, should be the one working as hard as he could to find out what had happened to him.

I couldn't help but remember that he wouldn't tell me the cause of the falling out. All he said was it wasn't something big and dramatic. It was as if he thought that fully excused the circumstances. Like it meant somehow there was less significance in the fact that they used to be friends if their no longer being friends wasn't an explosive story.

Trying to force those thoughts out of my mind, I walked quickly to the humanities building. The speed helped to keep me warm in the sharp early January air, but I also wanted to make sure I arrived at the class early so I didn't cause a disruption walking in.

Part of me expected to see another demonstration in front of the building when I arrived, but everything looked calm, normal, like nothing was going on. I went inside and followed the familiar path to the room Sydney had told me. I'd had several classes in that room during my years here. I got a wave of nostalgia as I walked into the room and slipped to the back to sit at the furthest corner desk.

Apparently, I didn't blend in at all because the moment Asher Vance walked into the class, his eyes locked on me and he flashed a smile.

"Agent Thorne," he said. "Just couldn't resist doing a bit of studying while back on your home campus?"

"I am feeling a little bit of panic that I don't have my backpack or homework assignment," I joked. "I hope you don't mind me sitting in. I'm just curious about what's going on in the class."

He held his hands out like he was opening up the room to me and raised his eyebrows a bit. "I don't see why not. You might find it interesting."

The rest of the seats rapidly filled with students as Asher wrote across the large whiteboard on the front wall of the large classroom. The seats were arranged on several tiers like a small amphitheater, providing a clear look at everyone. Without bothering to turn around to look at the students or greet them in any way, Asher started his lecture.

"Last class we started talking about the murders that have recently occurred on and around campus and stepped into the role of investigators for the case. We're going to be taking apart each step of an investigation, evaluating evidence, and discussing theories and possibilities. I warn you now as I did before. We are talking about actual murder. Real people. This is not abstract or something that was thought up for your textbook. It isn't neatly put aside in a record somewhere, safely solved and kept at a distance for you to explore without having to make any real connection to it.

"This is actually happening. Right now as we speak. This will not be easy, but it will be the most influential and formative educational experience you will have if you are actually serious about pursuing a career in law enforcement or criminal psychology. If you don't want to be a part of it or are not intent on being serious about this, then you need to leave now. This is not playtime."

He paused and turned to face the class like he was waiting for someone to stand up and walk out of the classroom. When no one did, he nodded and continued.

"The first steps in the investigation have already happened. The bodies have been found, and initial evidence has been collected. The victims have been identified, and those with close relationships with them have been spoken to by investigators. But the truth is, with two victims that seemingly have no connection to each other, the likelihood of a family member or a friend being able to provide the information necessary to completely solve this case is extremely unlikely. Not to say that they can't give some insight that will help with details like tracking their movements or understanding their current state of mind. It's just a simple reality that multiple victims without clear links generally mean there is something far bigger and more complex at play.

"Which means having to look for other connections and other clues that could provide that level of insight. When it comes to these cases, we find that in the passages in the books that have become synonymous with the killer's signature. That in and of itself is an interesting concept. One that I want to talk about today. What is the signature of a killer, and why does it matter? And when it comes to killings like this, is the signature simply a way to claim responsibility for a kill and create a persona, or is it an important piece of evidence that can be used to follow the crimes and track the killer?" he asked.

Already I was feeling less comfortable with this situation than I was when Sydney had first confirmed that Asher had apparently tossed away his syllabus for the semester in favor of using an ongoing case as a teaching aid. He was venturing very close to calling the students to make assumptions and jump to conclusions about the evidence that had been collected and shared by the media, which I already knew to be limited. There were pieces of it, including the specific passages themselves, that were being kept confidential, which meant he didn't have all the information needed to fully analyze the case. Yet the students were rattling off theories and ideas, bouncing off what he was saying and deducing things I could easily see leading down the path of another accusation.

As much as I wanted to interject several times throughout the lecture, I bit my tongue and forced myself to stay out of it. There were mistakes and wild leaps I absolutely wanted to correct, but I didn't want to offer any more fuel.

When the class finally ended, I lingered behind, waiting for the students to leave. A few of them stopped by to speak to the professor for a couple of minutes, but finally, everyone left and it was just the two of us. He finished packing items back into his bag and glanced up like he was just noticing I was still there.

"What did you think, Callan?" he asked.

"Honestly, I'm surprised. I thought we were in agreement when we spoke in Professor Campano's classroom. You seem to understand that talking about this and getting the kids too involved in it wasn't a good idea," I said.

"I know that's what we said, but I had a change of heart. After that conversation, I heard some of the other students talking about the case and how out of control and afraid it was making them feel. Once again one of them suggested the class should pick it up and study it as it unfolded. They approached me about it and said they thought it was a unique opportunity that would be a waste if we didn't take it. I thought about it and decided they were right.

"Not only does doing this give them the chance to talk through what they are experiencing in a constructive way, it is invaluable for their academic development. Discussing this case and going through the steps of an investigation is an ideal way for them to really understand the process in a safe context."

"That's the thing," I said. "I don't feel like this really is a safe context considering it's happening right at this moment. Like you said, this isn't some abstract case. It isn't something that happened before and you're just talking about it now. Or even something that's happening in another place. This is happening right here, right now. I just don't feel that it—"

"With all due respect, Agent, that isn't really any of my concern. You are here to investigate the murders, not dictate what the faculty of this school teaches or how they teach it. This is my class, and I have the right to teach whatever I want to and however I want to. It may be an unfortunate situation that this is happening right now, but that doesn't mean something beneficial can't come of it.

"Sitting by and not doing anything isn't going to do these students any good. They're not going to just pretend it isn't happening. Times have changed. I am raising up the next generation of people who are to protect the public and solve crimes as well as defend those who have suffered because of them. I have dedicated my entire career to this, and now I am really able to make a difference. I happen to know you took a similar class when you came to school here," Vance said.

My spine straightened. I knew I'd mentioned that I'd gone to school here, but I didn't say anything about taking a class like his.

"How did you know that?" I asked.

"I was a guest speaker in it. I consulted on that class. That was about eight years ago now? I don't forget names. And I don't forget faces. Especially those of students who are so eagerly invested in a class they try to answer nearly every question and have something to say at every second of every discussion. Maybe you recall that we studied the bus station bombing during that class. It wasn't happening at that exact moment, but it was recent, and it was very much local. You lapped it up. I had the opportunity to read your final paper for that class, and it was twice as long as the assignment dictated. You couldn't get enough of the chance to talk about that case and how it developed."

I was taken aback by what he said and felt called out by the observation. I didn't remember Asher Vance specifically, but looking back on the class, I did remember that there were guest speakers occasionally. I could only assume he was one of them. And the thing was, I knew he was absolutely right. I adored that class, largely because of the heavy emphasis on the bus station bombing that had captured my attention so intently during my freshman year.

If I were a student at the school right now, I would be completely wrapped up in trying to figure these murders out too. As differently as I looked at it from an investigator's perspective, I had to admit he was right in seeing it as an opportunity that could greatly enrich the education of these students. I felt like I was straddling a line. Half of me felt that way, but the other half was still pulled by my responsibility to protect the case.

We had been walking through the building as we talked and now were stepping out. As I was closing the door behind me, I noticed another man who also looked like a teacher heading into the building across the way. Beside me, Asher shook his head.

"I'm surprised to see him here," he said.

"Why? Who is that?" I asked.

"That's Laurence Harrison."

He said it as if I should place some significance on the name, but it didn't mean anything.

"I don't know how that is," I said.

"You don't? I would have thought it would have come out in the investigation already. He's another English professor. It's an open secret he was in a relationship with Danielle Scherer."

CHAPTER TEN

I STOOD IN SURPRISED SILENCE FOR A COUPLE OF SECONDS, PROCESSing the revelation. I had met and spoken with Nathan Garrett, Danielle's boyfriend. By all accounts, they were in a serious, stable relationship that had been going strong for several years. The idea that she was carrying on another relationship was unexpected enough. The thought of it being with her professor was truly startling. Nothing about what I'd learned about the girl would have led me to believe she would be involved in something like that.

I wanted to ask questions and get the details about the accusation, but I stopped myself. I didn't want Asher to put too much stock into the relationship or to have too much insight into how I was conducting my own investigation. Now that I knew about the class, I knew anything I said to him about my investigation or how the case was unfolding—even if it was only questions being asked about something he said—would end up being scribbled up on that whiteboard and presented for discussion. That meant they'd be spread around by the students, potentially compromising everything I was doing in the investigation and making it even more difficult to find the truth.

So instead of saying anything, I tucked the detail away, gave a nod of acknowledgment without any emotion attached, and said good night to the professor.

I checked my phone as I made my way back to my car. I'd missed a message from Tabitha. She'd been traveling for the last two weeks, exploring far-flung corners of the world, searching for hidden secrets and discoveries just waiting for her to stumble on them that would ease her unending thirst for connection with the distant past. These places bubbled over with intrigue and awe-inspiring hints at the accomplishments and lives of people who walked the earth thousands of years ago, but they were sorely lacking in the way of cell phone reception. This meant I frequently went long stretches without hearing from her and then faced a barrage of calls and messages when she made it back somewhere with a connection.

"Hey," I said when she answered my call.

"That doesn't sound like a person who's happy her best friend is going to be back in the States in a week," Tabitha said.

"I'm happy," I said.

I used my key fob to unlock my door and climbed in, turning the heater on and hunkering in my seat to wait for the warmth to kick in.

"Wow. Don't make me cry with your exuberance or anything," she said.

"I'm sorry. I really am happy. I'm just really distracted by the case I just started," I said.

"What's the case?" she asked.

"Two murders," I told her. "Guess where I just was."

"Where?"

"The humanities building."

"On campus?" she asked.

"That's the one."

Driving back toward my house had brought me right past the rebuilt bus station. Even now I could still see myself standing on the other side of the road watching Emma Griffin walk inside and pointing her out to Tabitha as she jogged up to drag me to class.

The next morning I was back at the library as soon as it opened. It was being carefully monitored with every book that had been returned thoroughly examined before going back on the shelves, and every book on the shelves being checked over carefully by at least two people to make sure nothing was missed. We were putting tremendous effort into doing all this without causing too much disruption. The students still needed access to the library for their studies, though many were avoiding it now because of the murders, but I was also intent on keeping as much of the investigation as possible confidential. I didn't want to risk the possibility that the killer was following my movements and could use that to stay a step ahead.

After a couple of hours, Jackson and I got coffee and went to the study room to go over what we had so far. I'd written each of the passages on an individual index card with a notation on the back to indicate in which order it was found and any information I'd gathered.

"This is the first one," I told Jackson, sliding the card toward him. "It was on the torn piece found before Warren's death."

"'Open your eyes and see what you can with them before they close forever,'" he read. "Anthony Doerr, *All the Light We Cannot See*."

I nodded. "That one seems like a fairly obvious warning about impending death. Which supports my theory that the torn pieces are a warning about an upcoming murder. It's the first indication that something is about to happen. This next one, though, doesn't really mean anything to me. It's the one that was underlined in blood. 'Anyone who ever gave you confidence, you owe them a lot.' That's in *Breakfast at Tiffany's* by Truman Capote."

"Yeah, I remember reading that. It had a lot fewer pancakes in it than I expected."

I looked over at him. Was Jackson trying to be funny? It was pretty difficult to tell considering he was still staring down at the index card without any change of expression.

"Okay. Well, that one does connect in a way to the second ripped paper. 'If you have the guts to be yourself, other people'll pay your price.' That's from *Rabbit, Run* by John Updike. I'm not familiar with that book, so I don't know what it means in the context of the original, but there's a similar idea going on in those two. Confidence, being courageous enough to be yourself, that's along the same lines. And you could say there's a link between the idea of owing somebody, like being grateful for what they've done, and having people being willing to 'pay your price,' or do as you want them to do," I said. "And here's our second underlined passage: 'Nowadays people know the price of everything and the value of nothing,' Oscar Wilde in *The Picture of Dorian Gray*. Owing someone, paying something, and the price of something. Lots of recurring themes here. Prices and values and things owed. But I don't think they're talking about money."

"Maybe it's a Ponzi scheme!" Jackson suddenly said, chuckling.

My eyes snapped to him. "All right, what is all this about? You would barely even speak to me yesterday, and now all of a sudden you're all jokes and giggles."

He shrugged. "I'm just in a good mood, I guess. Is that not allowed?"

I was confused by the sudden shift in his personality, but I really didn't have the luxury of time to contemplate it. I didn't encourage him with any more responses and went back to the passages.

"This last one really seems to apply to all these passages. Knowing the price but not putting any value on anything. Intrinsic value versus sentimental value. But what does that have to do with these people or their murders?" I asked, more to myself than actually to Jackson.

Because the torn piece of paper came first and then the next passage from the book was underlined in the victim's blood, it seemed to indicate a specific progression. The torn paper acted as an initial warning a murder was coming, then the underlined passage might have had something to do with why the victim was killed. But the longer I looked at it and read through the progression of the passages, the more I began to think that wasn't actually the purpose of those specific words.

"I think we're looking at this wrong. The torn passage is a warning, but not the first indication of a murder coming. This one was the first. It kicked off the whole thing. But the next three all have some sort of link to each other. The underlining means something. Not just indicating the words. That could be done in other ways. What if the underlined passage isn't about the victim that was already killed, but the next? Then the torn passage is the notes, the elaboration. Because there wasn't a victim before the first, all we got was the torn piece of paper. But then the underlined passage was the first indication of the next victim coming, and the torn paper further narrowed down that it was coming soon and the link between the victims."

"If you say so," Jackson said. "Honestly this all seems like a pretty huge leap to me. There still isn't any indication the victims are actually linked."

"Their blood was found smeared on the pages. As far as I'm concerned, that's linked enough for me."

It wasn't much. It didn't answer everything or inform exactly what path I was on now, but it was something. It put my feet on the ground and made me feel like there was finally a clear focus on what these passages could mean and how we could use them to find the killer.

CHAPTER ELEVEN

"Are you good to keep going here?" I asked, packing up a few things and heading for the door to the study room.

"Where are you going?' he asked.

"Remember the protest against Stephanie Campano? Those kids were trying to get her forced off campus because she's an English professor who has a thing for quotes from literature. Well, I got a little tidbit of information yesterday that I didn't put a lot of stock into, but now I am thinking I need to look into it a bit more. Asher Vance, the psychology professor? He told me it was fairly well known that our second victim, Danielle, was involved with a professor. Guess what that professor teaches."

"English?" he asked.

I lift my eyebrows at him in verification. "Keep in touch."

I found myself following the same path back to the building where I'd seen Professor Harrison. It brought me away from the sidewalks used by the other students around the side of the commons building and down a pathway that seemed longer than the conventional way but actually got me there much faster. Back when I was in school, it was a useful trick when I thought it was a good idea to schedule my classes far too close together and always found myself barely making it from one to the other through an entire semester.

I realized as I approached the building that I had seen the professor going inside but didn't actually know what classroom he was headed to—or even if that was a building he generally taught in or if he was just stopping by when we caught sight of him. Ducking inside to get into the heat, I pulled out my phone and went to the faculty registry to see if I could track him down. Schedules weren't available that would direct me to where he would be teaching at that time, but I was able to find out his office was in the building. I jogged up the steps to the fourth floor and made my way toward the office. As I walked past an open room, I caught sight of someone out of the corner of my eye and paused.

Standing inside the room, leaned over a table that seemed to be piled with student newsletters, was Laurence Harrison. I went to the door and knocked on it. He jumped slightly and looked up, blinking several times like he was trying to force away tears.

"Professor Harrison?" I asked.

His expression became confused, and he nodded, "Yes."

"Hi," I said, entering the room the rest of the way. "I'm Callan Thorne. I'm an agent with the FBI."

"What can I do for you?" he asked, busying himself with straightening the stacks of papers on the table.

I took note of the fact that he didn't seem surprised to have a special agent approaching him. That seemed to give credence to the rumor.

"I was hoping I could speak with you for a few minutes," I said. "Unless there's a better time."

He shook his head. "Now is as good as any. But I'm not sure if I can be of any help." He glanced over at me before carrying a stack of the papers over to another table. "That is, if I'm right in my assumption that you are here to talk about the murders. I can't really imagine any other reason the FBI would be on campus."

"That is why I'm here. But I'm surprised at how confident you are that you can't be of any help in my investigation considering the personal relationship you had with one of the victims," I said.

He paused, but didn't look at me.

"You did, didn't you? Danielle?"

I decided to approach it with confidence, as if I already knew about their relationship and was just waiting for him to confirm it rather than actually asking him if they were involved.

"I was hoping that wouldn't become a part of this," he finally said.

"You hoped the fact that you were having an affair with one of your students would come out during the investigation of her murder?" I asked incredulously.

He cringed, but when he looked at me, there was fire in his eyes. "I wasn't having an affair with her, and she wasn't my student. We were in a relationship. I'm not married and neither was she. This is exactly why I didn't want this to come to light. It is an extremely personal part of my life, and as you can imagine, it's also very painful for me. But beyond the emotions of the situation, there are certain practical issues at play as well. I'm sure you can appreciate me not wanting the administration to know about the relationship."

"I thought she wasn't your student."

"She wasn't. Not for the past few years. But that doesn't change the perceived impropriety of the relationship. Which I don't think I need to explain to you considering the way you brought it up. Even without knowing anything about us, or considering the fact that Danielle is… was… well past the age of adulthood, you were immediately judgmental of the possibility that we were involved. Your first inclination was to believe I somehow took advantage of her or am a predator based on my job," he said.

"I'm sorry," I said. "I had a knee-jerk reaction, and I shouldn't have. But that's why I came to talk to you before making it an official part of the investigation. The only person I've mentioned it to is my partner. I wanted the opportunity to get your insight into it before it turned into anything else."

"How did you find out?" he asked.

"I'd rather not discuss how I receive any of my information during investigations," I said.

"That makes sense. And I guess it doesn't really matter how you found out. At this point, you know. I hope that I can ask you for some discretion though. There are still people who could be hurt by this," he said.

"I will do the best I can not to bring this into any focus that it doesn't need to be in. But I can't promise you it won't come up if it seems to have relevance to the case. But that really depends entirely on what you can tell me about her and your relationship. I know it seems redundant and ridiculous, but I'm going to start with coming right out and asking you. Did you have anything to do with Danielle's death?"

"Absolutely not. I would never have hurt her. I know that our relationship looks bad. I think most people know by now that when a woman is murdered, the first person they look at is the romantic partner because that's who did it most of the time. So it makes sense that I would look suspicious just by that merit. The fact that there are books involved and I'm an English professor probably makes people think I am a suspect as well, even if that is a trite and incredibly on-the-nose modus operandi for someone in my field," he said.

"That's true," I said. "But just because something is trite and seems extremely predictable doesn't mean it isn't accurate, Professor Harrison. That's the reason the concept of trite exists."

"Call me Laurie," he said. He let out a mirthless chuckle. "I suppose I should be careful with my literary references, shouldn't I? I guess it's just my luck my name reminds people immediately of *Little Women*." He looked at me with a worried expression. "But that wasn't another book, was it?"

"I can't…" I started, but stopped when he held up his hands.

"You can't tell me. I know. Just for the record, I don't teach literature. I teach composition and creative writing," he said.

"If you teach composition and creative writing, why is Stephanie Campano the head of the writing club when she teaches literature?" I asked.

"It's as simple as she was available," he said. "There wasn't a club like that available on campus, and she decided to take it on when a student suggested it. Students have to have faculty backing and oversight in order to start any kind of club or organization. When that student first started the process, he approached me, but I had just agreed to a massive project and didn't have the time to devote to a new endeavor like that. I suggested they could talk to Stephanie about it.

"I don't know her very well on a personal level, but I do know that she is very dedicated and well-liked. I have the utmost and professional trust and respect for her, and I felt she would be the ideal mentor for students wanting to explore creative writing on a deeper level than that they get just in class."

"You mentioned that Danielle isn't your student anymore. Is that how you met?" I asked.

"Yes. She was my student early in her undergraduate studies. She was extremely promising as a writer, and I really enjoyed teaching her. She took several of my courses until she had taken everything available, and we parted ways as professors do with their students. Then a couple of years ago, I ran into her at the coffee shop where she worked. It was a really pleasant surprise to see her. We got to talking and ended up forming a friendship. Eventually, that turned into more.

"Like I said, she was very much an adult when our relationship became romantic. I had absolutely no inclinations toward her when I was teaching her. Nothing beyond recognizing a significant talent and hoping she would continue on with it. My feelings for her didn't start until we had already been spending time together after reconnecting. But despite that, I recognize it looks bad. It could damage my reputation regardless of the reality of the situation. I don't want that to happen. And I don't want people thinking badly about Danielle or anybody's feelings to get hurt because of our relationship.

"I really believed we had a future together. That's what I need you to understand. She wasn't a fling. She wasn't an affair, as you put it. There really wasn't that much of an age difference between us. Less than ten years. That might seem like a lot for a teenager, but not for a full-grown adult. I know there were obstacles. And there were things that we needed to figure out. But I fully planned on being with her. And I had absolutely nothing to do with her death. I can give you pictures and contact information for the event I was at the night she was killed. She was supposed to be with me that night. I was waiting for her. She never made it."

"You said you reconnected at a coffee shop. Is this somewhere people might have seen you together?" I asked.

"Absolutely. It's a very popular spot with students as well as people who live around campus. We had to be very careful and discreet anytime I was there. I thought about not going back at all, but she had started working there relatively recently, and I had been going to that shop for years. We just hadn't run into each other. We decided it would have looked more obvious if I just suddenly stopped going. Instead, we had to try not to call attention to anything when I was there. Apparently, we weren't convincing, or someone saw us together at another time."

"Have you heard that there were rumors going around about the two of you? You didn't seem particularly surprised when you heard I am with the FBI. With murders happening so close to campus and involving the library, I guess it isn't that big of a leap that you would see investigators around, but there are a lot of people on campus. You seemed far too resigned to the idea that someone would come to talk to you eventually. Even if you didn't want the information to come out," I said.

"I was hoping I was being too sensitive, but over the last several months, I heard a few fleeting comments that suggested people had caught on to our relationship. No one said anything to me outright or confronted me about it or anything, and Danielle wasn't upset about it. But I was aware that things were being said about us."

He stopped and drew in a deep breath as if suddenly overcome with emotion. Flattening his hand on the papers in front of him, he let out a shuddering exhale that held far more than any words he could have said to me. In that moment, I could feel his devastation.

"She wrote a piece for the newsletter. She liked to rate things and have them printed under assumed names. It gave her anonymity, of course, but I think she just also liked kind of channeling the history of women writing fiction before it was respectable. They often chose different names to publish under."

"Another reference to *Little Women*?" I pointed out.

"I suppose it is. I should be chiding her about her piece, waiting to see that little impish smile when she told me she heard the first person on campus make a reference to reading it. No matter how many times she put her writing out into the world or how many times people talked about it, she never acknowledged her own gifts. She never felt like she was good enough. Even when she could see how people reacted to her words, she just couldn't bring herself to see herself as anything special.

"That always drove me mad. She is so incredible. In every way. Was. She *was* incredible. It's going to take a lot of getting used to saying that. I don't know what I'm going to do without her. I loved her. More than I could ever sufficiently express. And I hate that and not only was she taken from me this way, but I don't even get the chance to grieve the way everyone else does. I see everyone gathering around Nathan to comfort him and tell him that he's going to get through it. They're sharing stories and letting him work through everything he's feeling surrounded by other people. I'm alone. I truly had her heart, and I'm alone. It's just as well, I suppose. Our relationship was hidden. Mourning her might as well follow suit."

It seemed from the intense emotion he was grappling with that Laurie was far more likely to kill Nathan than the woman he was so in love with, but I had seen my fair share of killers who chose to destroy the people who meant the most to them rather than facing a life without them. Right now I didn't know enough about their relationship or what was actually going on in Danielle's life to fully trust what the professor was telling me.

THE GIRL AND THE SECRET PASSAGE

I asked him the name of the coffee shop Danielle was working at, and instantly recognized it. I was familiar with the shop, but I never really paid attention to anyone working there, so I didn't know if I had ever crossed paths with Danielle. I decided to go to the shop and speak with her coworkers to find out more about her and her life beyond the campus.

CHAPTER TWELVE

Pretty much as I expected, everyone who had worked with Danielle at the coffee shop had wonderful things to say about her. I was almost hoping to find someone who had something less than flattering to say about her. Not because I didn't like the idea of such an exceptional person, but because not being able to find anyone with something bad to say about her presented me with an uncomfortable dichotomy. Someone this wonderful, this beloved by the people around her, with so much potential and such a bright future ahead, gave me both no one to suspect and everyone to suspect.

She was the type of person no one could imagine anyone wanting to hurt, yet that was often the exact person who was targeted. The fact that the one flaw she seemed to have was her romantic indiscretion only escalated that. Her death could have been the result of jealousy or of envy. Two concepts painfully and grotesquely intertwined like tangled vines. One the desperate need to have, the other the desperate need to keep.

I spent some time at the coffee shop just listening to the people who knew Danielle talk about her. Coworkers and regular customers alike talked about her as being warm, friendly, and kind. They said she wanted everyone to be happy. At the same time, she could be very quiet, shy, and sensitive. She wasn't outgoing and boisterous. Not the life of the party or one who was known to get out and socialize very often. But those who had gotten close to her thought of her as someone they could trust. Someone they could talk to about anything and not feel judged or looked down on.

She saw something in everybody.

I tried to think back to the times I had been in the shop to figure out whether Danielle had ever served me when I came in for a cup, but I couldn't place her. The truth was, I was usually too hurried or distracted to really pay attention to the person helping me. Not that I was openly rude. At least I tried not to be. But I wasn't a customer who chatted with the person behind the counter or sat at the coffee shop leisurely enjoying my drink. I was glad for the time that I had talking to the people who did know her. It helped me to feel more connected to Danielle.

As much as I wanted to just keep the conversation pleasant and let them enjoy sharing the happy memories of Danielle, I knew I had to push harder to find the details I really needed.

"Can any of you tell me anything about a professor Danielle might have been seeing?" I asked.

The four people behind the counter and the one who had already clocked out but was sitting on one of the high stools to carry on the conversation looked confused. They shook their heads.

"A professor? Like somebody at the school? No," one of the baristas said.

"She never talked about anybody older or anybody at the school," one of them said.

I took note of a reluctant hint in her voice. I couldn't tell if it was because she knew something and didn't want to talk about it, or if just the thought of conjecturing about Danielle's romantic life made her that uncomfortable.

"Why would she?" the cook sitting at the counter beside me eating an incredible-looking sandwich asked, picking up a napkin and wiping his mouth. "She had Nathan. They had been together since, what, the dawn of time?"

"Maybe not quite that long," another of the girls behind the counter said with a slight laugh. "But it definitely felt like it. I knew her a long time before she started working here, and she and Nathan had been together for a while before we even met."

"And it seemed like they were happy together?" I asked.

"Unbelievably so," she said.

"It was kind of disgusting," the cook added. "They were that couple that stared at each other all the time and couldn't stop holding hands and calling each other by squishy little nicknames."

A barista named Tanis, whom I knew tangentially and didn't realize worked there until I came in, nodded. "But who could blame her? Nathan is pretty much the perfect guy. If that even exists. In fact, he might be the only one on earth. He's gorgeous. He's sweet. He's attentive. He looks at her like the sun rises and sets with her. She was constantly talking about the amazing things that he did for her, and he would come in here to visit and bring her food from her favorite restaurant or flowers he saw that made him think of her. It was like he couldn't stand to be away from her."

"They didn't live together," I said. "Do you know why?"

"I asked her about that one time," Tanis said. "They've been together for so many years, and it just seemed like they would live together. That's just the natural thing, right? I don't think I've ever known anybody who has been together as long as they have who didn't live together. But Danielle was really traditional and old-fashioned in a lot of ways. Even though it would have been a lot easier for both of them to afford living in the city if they were sharing all the expenses, it meant a lot to her that they didn't live together until they were married. They weren't engaged, but it was a foregone conclusion that they would be married one day. And I think she was just really looking forward to that monumental change where they would finally really share their life together."

"That's beautiful," I said.

"Oh my gosh," one of the others behind the counter suddenly said. "Do you remember that time Nathan came in on Valentine's Day dressed as Romeo, and she pointed out how that wasn't exactly the best choice of a costume for someone wanting to be romantic?"

I felt a slightly sick feeling in my stomach at the reference, but none of them seemed to notice. Instead, they laughed, their minds going to the humor of the memory rather than the dark implications. They launched into more stories about the couple, lavishing praise on Nathan and their incredible relationship. All of them only had gushing things to say, so much so that it almost seemed put on. Like they were extending too much effort to craft this image of perfection. Perhaps I was being cynical, but they were all so glowingly adoring of both of them it was suspicious. Like things were far too good to actually be real and maybe these people, some of the closest to Danielle, were covering something up.

"I think there's a picture of that up on the wall still," Tanis said. "Here, let me show you."

I realized I'd missed part of the story they were telling me and wasn't sure what I was supposed to be looking at when she led me over to the wall at the back of the coffee shop. In keeping with the intense art focus of Richmond, the entire wall acted as one large evolving art installation. Employees and customers alike were encouraged to add sketches, paintings, and photographs of the shop and the people in it to create a collage that was constantly changing. It was a record of the memories made within the shop but had also become a way for people to mark major moments in their lives. There were doodles on napkins from first dates. Sketches from breakups. Photographs of people dressed alike. Even proposals commemorated in tiny art.

It was truly moving, and I probably could have stood there for hours just taking everything in if it wasn't for the one photograph at the edge of the wall that caught my attention and drew me toward it. Part of it was covered by a sketch next to it, but the visible portion was very clearly Danielle. She was sitting at one of the tables by the window, her elbows resting in front of her as she leaned slightly toward the person across from her. Outside the window fall leaves swirled in a breeze, creating a perfect moment caught in the frame.

I wasn't interested in the artistic merit of the photograph or why it was taken. What mattered was what I couldn't see. I moved the sketch aside to see who Danielle was in such an intent conversation with.

Warren Mason.

"Didn't she look beautiful? She completely missed the point of the whole thing, but she looked great," Tanis said.

"What?" I asked, looking at her.

She gave me a questioning lift of her eyebrow and pointed at a pencil sketch in front of her. "An artist did this of Danielle on Halloween a couple years ago when we all decided to go as toy aisle rejects. She thought she'd dressed up as a messed-up Barbie doll but ended up looking amazing. Even when she tried to do something wrong, she couldn't manage to do it."

The words rang in my ears, taking on a significance I was sure Tanis didn't actually intend. I pointed out the photograph.

"Do you remember when this was taken?" I asked.

She looked at it for a second, then shook her head. "No. I mean, there are leaves in the background, and her hair was short. Her hair was really long, but then she donated it, so it was up to her shoulders. So probably just a couple months ago. Around Thanksgiving probably. Why?"

"Don't you know who that is sitting at the table with her?" I asked.

She examined it again, but no recognition crossed her eyes. "No."

"It's Warren Mason. The man who was murdered a couple days before Danielle."

Tanis's eyes widened, and she drew in a sharp breath.

"What's wrong?" the cook asked.

"This picture," Tanis said, pulling the photograph down. "Do you know when it was taken? Or who took it?"

She carried it over to the counter so the others could get a look at it. Customers in two of the booths watched, and I wished the employees would be a bit more subtle. I was trying to contain the rumors already swirling around. The last thing I needed was more stemming from the coffee shop.

"No one recognizes it," Tanis told me, holding the picture out. "Do you want to take it with you?"

"That would be great, if you don't mind."

I left the coffee shop with the picture in my satchel and more questions on my mind. Everyone I spoke to could do nothing but heap praise and adulation on Danielle, but little cracks were starting to show. This girl was supposed to be sweet and caring, in a fabulous relationship with the perfect guy. Yet she had a relationship going with a professor at her school who used to teach her and seemed to be fairly cozy with a man who would later become a fellow murder victim.

I needed to find out more about Warren. I'd done my best to speak to his sister, but she hadn't given me much. She didn't live in town, and while they were close, she admitted they weren't the kind of siblings that delved deep into each other's personal lives. I hoped she was just processing through her grief and would have more to tell me later, but for now, that was all I had.

Except for Jackson.

He'd already given me the brush-off when it came to talking about Warren and what happened between the two of them, but I couldn't just let it go. I needed to know what he could tell me about the man and about what led to the breakdown of their friendship. From what I was told, the two of them were extremely close for a time. Whatever came between them had to be serious. I wanted to know what it was.

"I thought we already decided that my friendship with him years ago doesn't have anything to do with what's going on now and we weren't going to discuss it," he said later when I got back to the library.

"I didn't actually say we weren't going to discuss it," I said. "Just that I agreed it wasn't enough to have you removed from the case. You know a murder victim. Which means you have insight into his personality and how he handles friendships. Something happened between the two of you that stopped you from being friends."

"Exactly. It stopped us from being friends. A long time ago. I don't know a murder victim. I knew one. More than ten years ago. A lot changes in a decade. I have no idea about what type of person he became in that time. Me not liking the person he was becoming is what caused our falling out," Jackson said.

Any hint of the humor that had been in him earlier was now gone.

"But you can tell me about who he used to be. Why did you end up friends in the first place?" I asked.

"We were in a couple of classes together. And isn't that how most people become friends in college? At the time he was funny and outgoing. He was the kind of guy everybody gravitated toward. He was smart but didn't always know exactly what he wanted. I was a lot like that at the time too. I bounced around from major to major. I barely even remember school. But Warren wanted to do it all. He talked about starting a business and all the success he was going to have. Things were really good between us until they weren't. That's all I have to say about it," he said.

When I was back home later, I tried to take everything Jackson had told me and find out more about Warren. It really hadn't been much, not enough to illuminate anything new about him. Other than his sister, there wasn't any family to reach out to. He was self-employed, which showed he had taken seriously what he had told Jackson and actually achieved it. It also meant there were no coworkers to talk to. There just wasn't much to go on, including not being able to find any other connections with Danielle.

I went back to my notes about the book passages, reading them over and over trying to understand them. The concept of "price" seemed to connect the two of them because of the fact that she sold him coffee, though that was so surface-level and direct it seemed silly. She was also known to be a kind, beautiful person, but also somewhat shy and always focused on trying to make the people around her happy. That connected somewhat to the quote about confidence and being herself. But all that just felt too simple. There was something more there, something that would link them to the killer, but I couldn't find it.

CHAPTER THIRTEEN

I was back in the criminal psychology classroom for Asher's next class. I sat in the same desk, again remaining silent and just listening in. Even though I had only been with the Bureau a short time, I had already learned that there are two parts to investigating murder. There is the active role—actually being out in the field doing research, conducting interviews, chasing down leads. But then there is the more passive side—when it is better to take a step back and focus on observation. How people act and the things they say when they don't think they are directly involved in the investigation can often be more illuminating than what they offer when they are questioned.

It was obvious the situation was deeply affecting the students, and they were serious about talking it through and letting their opinions and beliefs on the issue be heard. But even with the clear drive and the good ideas floating around the discussion, there was nothing monumental coming out of the class.

All the students agreed the victims weren't random. They had to have something to do with each other and the killer; it just wasn't clear at the moment what it was. One student piped up to bemoan the lack of video evidence and proclaim that it was irresponsible and negligent of the school not to have more security available throughout campus. This instantly sparked a heated conversation about the ethical implications of constant surveillance through security video and audio, and what that means for living in a free society.

That conversation immediately got me thinking about the bus station explosion again and how I interpreted the entire situation at the time. I remembered my instant fascination with the case. It was obvious some of the fascination came simply because of the proximity. I was right there when it happened, so I was drawn to watching it all unfold. But it was undeniable that my own interest—as well as that of other people on campus, in town, and in the country at large—was also fueled by the powerful effect of the prominent social media element. I could still clearly remember Mary Preston's video footage and brief clips from other people being played repeatedly, interspliced with security images from outside the station.

It was widely disseminated during the investigation through media coverage, but also through people sharing it from one person to the next. At the time I was eager for all those images and every detail I could. When I was able to pull myself out of that hunger for the next little shred of information though, there was also a bit of an ick factor. These intensely private, horrifying moments were being recorded and then were just handed out to people, put up on display like entertainment. It felt wrong. And yet, they proved crucial to the case. It was through one of those bits of video that Emma Griffin found a key image that ended up unlocking not just that case, but a far larger, more complex web.

"What I don't understand is why the library is being left open," a student named Jeffrey said angrily. "It should have been shut down as soon as this started."

"Why?" another student whose name I hadn't caught yet asked. "It isn't like they were killed there or their bodies were found there."

"Exactly," Anthony said. "If every place where a clue to a crime was found ended up getting shut down, society would be completely crippled."

"People still have to function, and the library is important to everybody here on campus," somebody else said.

"But don't you think it's disrespectful?" Jeffrey asked. "It's a place where not just evidence of a crime showed up, but it's almost like a memorial."

A girl named Corrine rolled her eyes. "Again, not every place that has to do with a crime has to be revered."

"It's not about it being revered," Sydney pointed out. "And honestly, I don't think it matters so much about showing respect for the fact that the books were found there. That's not really the point. I'm wondering more about the logistics of the investigation. With the library open, doesn't that make it possible to compromise the scene? Take away the possibility of evidence being found?"

"I think that ship sailed when a couple thousand students tromped through the space before the books were found," Asher pointed out. "But I understand your thought process. It does seem like there's some disagreement among our investigators about how locations pertinent to the case should be handled. Is it practical or even beneficial for a place where evidence was found to be cut off from its normal use just because evidence was found there? If the student hadn't returned the book with the torn page to the library and instead it was somehow found in his room by his roommate, would that mean the entire dorm should be shut down? Would it somehow alter what's seen as important when looking at this case?"

"But that isn't what happened. The books were found in the library. And that student was questioned, right?" Anthony asked.

"I don't have an answer for that. But we are fortunate enough to have a pretty exceptional resource right at our fingertips. Agent Thorne, can you give us some insight about that?" Asher asked, looking directly at me.

I was surprised to be put on the spot like that and hoped he could see the displeasure on my face without it being too obvious to the students. I'd come to the class with the intention just of listening, not becoming a part of it.

"I'm sure all of you here understand I'm not at liberty to discuss specifics of the investigation." I felt like I had repeated that sentiment more during this case than I had ever needed to in any of my previous investigations. "But since I am sure he's already discussed it with people, yes, of course, that student was questioned in relation to the book he returned to the library. As for why the library remains open during the investigation, the theories that were already presented here are accurate. The library is a necessary resource for the students on campus. Because of the foot traffic that goes through that building all the time, it isn't plausible to consider it a preservable crime scene."

"That seems like a complete cop-out," Corinne said. "Just because people have gone through the library or touched things doesn't mean there can't be evidence found. Murders have been solved based on evidence found in landfills or fingerprints lifted off of rocks in public parks. I would venture to say both of those locations have fairly heavy traffic and interference with other elements."

"She isn't telling you everything," Sydney said. "You honestly think she's going to sit there and give you all the details of her investigation? She literally just said she can't talk about specifics. There's something else going on in that building that nobody is talking about."

"We deserve to know," Jeffrey said. "If there's some sort of threat or if something else is going on this campus, everybody here has the right to that information."

"You don't have the right to anything when it comes to a murder investigation," Anthony said. "Investigators can do whatever they want as long as it gets them to the answers."

I waited for Professor Vance to step in and temper what was becoming another heated exchange, but he remained silent at the front of the classroom. There was a slight smirk on his face like he was amused by how much the discussion was riling up the students.

"Every investigation is different," I said, lifting my voice above the bickering students. "But in every investigation, there are pieces of information that are kept confidential. This might be evidence that was found, details that have come to light, or approaches the investigators are taking. It's not a matter of being deceitful or trying to cover things up. The library is being searched. That's obvious. Anyone who has gone into the library since this started can see that there are people taking the books off the shelves to check them over. That is not being hidden from anyone. While this is happening, students are still allowed to access the building and use the books like always. It's a matter of balancing what's best for everyone, the people involved in the case and those just existing within the periphery of it."

"I am much more than existing on the periphery of this case," a student who had been quiet for nearly all of both classes I sat in suddenly said. "That might be the way other people look at it, but it's not for me. Danielle was one of my best friends. I can't even look at that library without feeling sick. To know somebody killed her, then took her blood and smeared it in a book is horrifying in a way I can't describe. That library being open..." He stopped and shook his head, looking down at his hands for a second. "I just think it's too soon for people to act like everything is normal."

⁓

As class ended, I lingered back again to talk to Asher. He didn't smile at me as I approached.

"Yes, Callan?" he said in an almost-resigned tone, like I was bothering him. "I am in a hurry this evening, so I'll need you to walk with me if you need to talk about something."

As though he wanted to emphasize his need to rush, he shoved everything into his bag and was already heading toward the door almost before he finished the sentence.

"I'd appreciate it if you didn't call me out like that again," I said as we headed down the hallway.

"Call you out?" he asked. "Oh. You mean involved you in the discussion. You did show up to my class for a second time, Callan. You didn't ask me if you could be there or tell me it was part of your investigation. You just showed up. I took that to mean you were interested in what we had to say and would be willing to be a part of it."

"I'm not a student," I said. "I didn't need your permission to sit in on your class. You put me in a very awkward position."

"By asking your professional insight?" he asked. "I would think that would be exactly what you would want me to do when a student asked a question. I don't have the professional expertise you do or the closeness to the case. I figured you would be able to give a more concise and reliable answer."

"That conversation was getting completely out of hand. It's exactly what I warned you about the first time we talked about this class. Those students were coming up with their own explanations for things and placing emphasis and meaning where they didn't need to be. That's going to end up filtering out to other people and causing serious problems," I said.

"It was just a classroom discussion," he said dismissively. "They are sharing their ideas and developing new ones. That's the entire purpose of higher education."

"That doesn't apply when it comes to potentially compromising the investigation into two murders," I said.

"We aren't compromising anything. We're just discussing facts of a situation. No one here is going to try to take down the killer ourselves," he said. "It's no different from any random group of people discussing it anywhere."

I was bothered by how unaffected he seemed, like he was thinking of the case only as something to teach about rather than a real situation. He didn't seem to care how the conversations he was leading with his students could genuinely impact the investigation, particularly when what was supposed to be ideas and theories started spiraling into accusations.

"I really do need to be going," he said when we got outside. "I have a standing appointment at eight o'clock and I can't be late. Have a good evening, Agent."

I watched him leave, torn between my view of what was happening as an investigator and the part of me that was still the student engrossed in the case unfolding around me. Feeling discouraged, I got in my car and found myself drawn to the rebuilt bus station.

CHAPTER FOURTEEN

The bus station was dark and quiet. It wasn't really a bus station anymore. The station closed about a year before, and the building was left to sit empty, taking up a massive chunk of the road and offering nothing but a place for transients to sleep in sheltered doorways and graffiti artists to practice their tags. The city promised big ideas for the building and the area around it, bandying around thoughts of a pocket park, a community center, an art gallery, or a crisis center. But for now, it was just the empty shell of what it once had been. No buses sat in the bays. The doors were chained and locked. Black-and-white spray paint had been used to obscure the windows so the curious couldn't peer inside.

Of course, that only made me more curious. If it was just an abandoned bus station, why the need to conceal the inside? What could be in there that needed to be hidden from curious eyes?

In the more logical part of my brain, I knew the building could be repurposed as storage for any number of things, including expensive construction equipment and materials intended for use in the future development of the building. But there was another voice in my head, a quieter but more insistent one far in the back that always reminded me of the darkness that lurked inside people, the possibilities in the shadows. An empty building was a haven for the unwanted, the cast aside, and the willfully othered. The ones who skirted society rather than joined it.

Blocking the windows left enough questions of whether there were authorities or surveillance inside to keep some of them out. But it also granted anonymity and cover to those who ventured inside anyway.

The building hadn't been blocked off with a fence, so I walked across the cracked parking lot to the double glass doors that used to open up into a vestibule and then into the main portion of the building. The doors were set back a couple of feet, creating an alcove that would keep at least the bite of the wind off someone whose circumstances left them sleeping on the streets tonight. I tried not to let my mind wander to the added reality that the tile and concrete building would also provide something to put their back against, offering them a least a little bit of protection.

Some of the spray paint had flaked off the inside of the glass, and I cupped my hands to peer inside. The darkness around me made it possible to see the little glimmer of emergency lights inside. Like most buildings left empty in areas that were still being used, the station still had power running to it. That provided security and lighting as well as made it easier to handle emergencies if something were to happen, like a fire breaking out inside.

Other than the little lights glowing over entrances, there was little to see. I didn't notice any equipment or tools and likewise didn't see any suspicious movement or shapes in the dim interior. Nothing had changed since the last time I'd been there. It wasn't a place I went to on a daily basis, but I found myself drawn to it when I needed to think or wanted a clear reminder of how my career really started. When I was frustrated or felt like I'd lost my way in an investigation, I'd come to the bus station and remember the experience of watching Emma Griffin climb out of that black car and walk into the charred ruins. It was a moment that changed my life and my future. And sometimes I just needed to put myself back there.

I was still peering through the doors when my phone rang. I was surprised to see Jackson's name on the screen.

"Hey," I said.

"Where are you?" he asked.

"I'm actually at the bus station," I said.

"The bus station? Are you going somewhere?" he asked.

"Wow, I hope not, considering this station has been defunct for a year. I'd have to wait for a while for a bus to come by," I said.

"Oh, that station. I'm five minutes away. I'll be right there," he said.

Before I could question why he wanted to come or tell him I was getting ready to leave, he hung up. It felt a bit awkward to stand there in front of the station waiting for him. I could only imagine what the cars driving by were thinking. Headlights swept over me, and my first instinct was that a squad car was responding to somebody's concerned 911 call about a suspicious woman lurking around the bus station. Again, it wouldn't be the first time.

Fortunately, a flash of my FBI badge and a quick explanation were enough to ward off any attempts at taking me in. Not to say I hadn't encountered a couple of officers who seemed like they wanted to, if only for the break from their nightly rounds to bring me to the station and then immediately let me loose.

As it turned out, that wasn't going to be the night for that either. The car parked, and Jackson got out. I was blowing warm breath into my hands to thaw the cold that had seeped through my gloves when I met him in the middle of the parking lot.

"Why did I stand here freezing for you to come meet me?" I asked. "I thought you were far too busy in the evenings to have anything to do with the investigation."

"I didn't necessarily say I was too busy in the evenings. Just that I had a life outside of the investigation," he said.

"But not tonight?" I asked.

"Not tonight. I thought we could talk about what you found out at the coffee shop and the class."

I gave half a shrug. "All right. But I'm not standing in the middle of the parking lot to do it."

Jackson chuckled and nodded. "All right. Well, I'm starving. So how do some nighttime pancakes sound?"

"Still thinking about *Breakfast at Tiffany's*?" I asked.

"I got it into my head, and now it won't go away," he said. "And I hear Third Street has a special going on. Let's go find out if I can eat an eighteen-inch stack of pancakes."

"I mean, if you can't, I can," I said. "That's like a leisurely Sunday morning brunch for me."

"Is that a challenge?" he asked.

"I mean, no," I said. "That's exactly what I mean. It's just what I eat. That was the point of that whole statement."

He looked at my blank expression for a beat. Now it was his turn to be confused as to whether I was joking or not.

"We'll see," he said. "Want a ride?"

"I'll follow you. I don't think parking enforcement would love me leaving my car there for long," I said.

In truth, it was more than just not being completely confident about the legality of my parking job. I, as Tabitha would put it, had a thing about riding in cars with other people behind the wheel. Jackson and I seemed to have somehow stumbled into a better rapport, and I knew I should place my trust in him simply because he was my partner in the case, but I still didn't want to be in his car with him in control. One day maybe I would get over it.

And maybe I never would.

The diner was a long-standing mainstay in Richmond and was often busier in the middle of the night than it was during the day. Everyone from students cramming for tests and finishing up projects, to travelers passing through, to revelers streaming out of the nightclubs and bars made their way to Third Street to fall face-first into massive plates of traditional greasy spoon food served alongside a few more unique items with a bit of local flair.

It wasn't quite late enough for the masses to arrive, so Jackson and I had our choice of seating. We picked a booth closer to the back of the restaurant. He immediately ordered a cup of coffee while I asked for hot tea. The waitress handed us menus and disappeared into the back.

"So why were you hanging out at a closed bus stop?" he asked. "Did I interrupt some sort of clandestine meeting?"

I raised an eyebrow at him. "Are you asking me if I abandoned a potential witness with information about the case to have pancakes with you, or if I decided that was the best spot to meet up with a date?"

"Would you admit to either?" he asked with a hint of that humor that had started showing up in the library.

"You aren't that lucky," I said. "And as it turns out, I'm not that interesting either. Going there helps me center myself."

"The closed bus station?" he asked. He sat back as the waitress returned with our drinks.

"Ready to order?" she asked.

We chose our food, and the waitress scooped up our barely read menus before walking away. Jackson gave a thoughtful frown as he reached for several packets of artificial sweetener and shook them.

"I guess everybody can find their zen in their own way," he said.

I made a face as he poured a sparkling cascade into his coffee and stirred it around.

"That stuff is going to kill you," I said. "Why don't you just put real sugar in it?"

"I have to watch my figure," he said. "Wouldn't want to be chasing a perp and get weighed down by all those calories."

Something told me Jackson didn't actually know how many calories were in sugar and was dumping the little blue packets into his coffee with the same kind of abandon he witnessed one of his parents or grandparents do when he was young.

"I'll stick with the honey," I said, adding a glistening spoonful to my tea from a jar sitting on the table.

The label bragged the honey inside was from a farm about an hour outside the city limits. It was the same farm where I used to visit the pumpkin patch when I was little.

"All right. Back to the bus station," he said.

"Right. Well, I wouldn't exactly say I go there to find zen. Like I said, it centers me. It keeps me focused. You know how some people carry around something like a matchbook from the restaurant they were eating in when they got their first job offer, or wear the same pair of socks when they are in the middle of an investigation? The bus station is that for me."

I told him about my experience with the bombing and finding such inspiration in Agent Emma Griffin.

"Of course I know who Emma Griffin is," he said when I asked if he was familiar with her. "Anybody in the Bureau around here better. She's handled some insane cases. And the fact that she's Agent Martinez's best friend doesn't hurt her prominence. Have you met her?"

"No. But I heard him talking to her on the phone once. That's a surreal moment. I mean, I'm not one to go starstruck over people, but she's impressive. She's the reason a lot of people joined the FBI. I know she is for me."

He makes a curious sounding, "hm."

"I think I always knew that I was going to end up doing something that had to do with law enforcement or victims' advocacy or something along those lines. Psychology. Forensics. But as soon as everything happened with the bus station and I started following her investigation, I knew that was what I wanted to do," I said. "And before you make this weird, it isn't like I have a shrine to her there or anything. I don't whisper to a picture of her at night or commemorate her birthday with a cupcake and a single candle every year."

I realized Jackson was staring at me, his spoon stopped in his mouth from where he was sucking the coffee off. He withdrew it slowly.

"That escalated kind of quickly," he said.

I sighed and took a sip of my tea. "Well, I have brothers."

I hoped that was enough of an explanation for him. It seemed to be because he didn't push any further. Our food arrived, and we thanked the waitress, then went to work pouring syrup over our pancakes and diving into the stacks.

"What about you?" I asked through my third mouthful of buttermilk perfection. "How did you get here?"

"Here, Richmond?" he asked.

"No. Here the FBI."

"Oh. Well, I was actually born here in the city. At the teaching hospital. I grew up around here but ended up leaving to go to college. I was in the middle of a city that has like nine colleges in it, and yet I decided to go out of state. Just because I thought it would be fun and that particular school caught my attention in high school. I didn't have a whole lot of direction though. I always kept my grades up enough so I didn't fail, and I enjoyed trying different things. I just couldn't really settle on any one specific thing for a few years. Then I just kind of stumbled into it," he said.

I blinked. "You just kind of stumbled into the FBI?"

"Yeah," he said.

"I don't think that's how it works," I said. "In fact, I think that's exactly the opposite of how it works."

"I didn't really plan it. I can't remember the exact chain of events that went into me deciding it was what I was going to pursue. It just kind of ended up that way," Jackson told me.

I felt a twinge of something at the base of my skull. Something about his answer bothered me. I remembered when Agent Martinez was talking about him right before I met him for the first time. He told me Jackson had always intended on being in law enforcement when he was younger and was then fascinated by profiling when he was in high school and started talking about the requirements to get into the Bureau, only to find out applicants had to be a minimum of twenty-three. That led him to a somewhat meandering path through college and then a few years as a police officer.

This seemed to contradict what Jackson was telling me now, leaving me feeling uneasy. We didn't know each other particularly well, and this had felt like a good step toward building the kind of connection we needed if we were going to solve this case. But it was tempered by his strange behavior and conflicting statements. It was almost like there was a past he was trying to cover up.

Before I could dig any further, my phone rang. I set down my fork and wiped my syrup-sticky fingers to take the phone out of my pocket. I thought it might be Tabitha calling. Instead, my heart sank when I saw Detective Tarrant's name. The call lasted less than ten seconds.

I gestured at the waitress and signaled for the check.

"What's going on?" Jackson asked.

"We have to go," I said, very aware of the other people in the diner.

"I'm not even halfway through my stack," he said.

The waitress arrived carrying boxes for our leftovers, and I tipped his plate into one. It took another to accommodate all the pancakes, but I got them all to fit. I added an extra drizzle of syrup, handed several bills to the waitress, and headed for the door.

"Callan, what's wrong? What's happening?" Jackson asked, chasing after me as I headed for my car.

"That was the detective," I told him. "Two more books have been found."

CHAPTER FIFTEEN

"THE BOOKS WERE FOUND IN TWO DIFFERENT USED BOOKSTORES in the city. Both locations are owned by the same people. The book with the torn page was found at the on-campus bookstore where students buy and sell their used textbooks. They're accustomed to books coming back with some damage, so they tried not to put too much thought into it when they noticed one of the books they were processing back into their system had a piece missing from one of the pages.

"They also own a general used-books bookstore off-campus. The book with the blood underline was found on a shelf that had been on display for a sidewalk sale. But it wasn't from their inventory. It had been placed there," Detective Tarrant told us when we arrived at the police department, ushering us into the room where she had both books sitting on a conference table.

"So whoever did this brought that book to the bookstore and slipped it into a shelf," I said.

"That wouldn't be all that difficult," Jackson said. "It's been cold out, so people are wearing coats and heavy jackets. It's not a very big book. They could have easily snuck it in from inside their coat."

"We've missed a victim. There's a body that we haven't found. And we have to find them," I said, feeling sick to my stomach that this happened under my watch. "Have you been able to interpret the torn paper to find the passage being highlighted?"

"No, I called you immediately when they came in. The only thing that's been done with the books is processing them for fingerprints," she said. She touched the cover of one of the books. "This one has the torn page. Mary Shelley. *Frankenstein*."

We immediately ran an internet search to find the exact copy of the book so we could locate the words. After twenty minutes of searching and comparisons, we were able to isolate the passage.

"'Beware; for I am fearless, and therefore powerful,'" I read. "How about the other one? The bloody passage?"

Detective Tarrant flipped through a copy of L. M. Montgomery's *Anne of Green Gables* and slid the book toward me when she'd settled on a specific page. "'Isn't it nice to think that tomorrow is a new day with no mistakes in it yet?'" She made an appreciative sound. "That says a mouthful."

"But what does it mean?" I asked. I whispered the words from the damaged page to myself several times, kind of trying to get them into my mind so something might come to the surface. "'Fearless and powerful.' That doesn't really mean anything. That could be anybody."

"What if it isn't the words?" Jackson asked. "I mean, not those words specifically. What if it's the book itself?"

"What do you mean?" I asked.

"*Frankenstein*," he said. "Maybe the clue is *Frankenstein*. Like a monster."

We thought for a few seconds, trying to decipher what that could mean.

"The creature mural?" Detective Tarrant suggested. "In the old neighborhood at the very edge of the city. There's that huge mural."

"It's a start," I said. "We're going to need a team with flashlights."

The cold always felt so much more intense at night. The darkness gave it a level of aggression, a more threatening nature that reminded you of your fragility and just how easily everything could go so wrong. The temperature had plummeted that night ever since I'd stood at the bus station. It felt like there was ice in the air as we walked across an old patch of scrub grass to the wall of what used to be a shop decades ago when this area of the city was vibrant and alive.

Now the majority of the buildings had been abandoned, the businesses closed, the people gone from the sidewalks. Nearby homes sagged in various stages of disrepair. A few barber shops, nail salons, shops, and a couple of minuscule ministries that presented themselves as churches but that always gave a predatory vibe had taken up residence in the shells of the former destinations. The one we were looking at then had once been a large music store.

There were also signs of the area being gradually rehabilitated. But true revival was far off. In the city archives, there were pictures of this area at its peak. One of them showed people gathered inside this building listening to records. Black-and-white slivers of time now faded into obscurity. The building was now boarded up. The faded sign for the shop was almost unreadable. Whitewashed cement block walls were now a pale shade of blue that on one side had been nearly fully obscured with an elaborate mural.

This was the way life was brought back to the neglected, tired corners of the city. Artists took up their paint like weapons and fought back against being forgotten, against the past being shoved down and people thrown away in the name of progress. Murals covered the city—from the ones like this that acted to remind anyone who saw it that the area existed, that there was still life there; to massive ones emblazoned on buildings in prominent spots to make bold statements that didn't require words; to tiny ones left like secrets the cement told the people who noticed them.

This particular one was a staggering piece I couldn't even begin to imagine creating. Graffiti tags and a couple of sharply applied signatures at the bottom corner suggested multiple artists contributed to the piece. Not all of them gave any acknowledgment of the artists who made them, which suggested this piece was part of a large collaborative that might have even been sponsored by an organization within the city.

Our flashlights swept over the surface of the mural, glowing on a complex assortment of creatures intertwined and flushed with fantastical colors. Snakes, dinosaurs, massive bats, turtles, ravens, and various other animals filled the wall. It was impressive. But there were no indications of murder around it. No body. No blood.

The team searched the entire area, trying to come up with anything. It was starting to feel like we were completely off on our interpretation when one of the officers Detective Tarrant sent with us came jogging up to me.

"Agent Thorne," he said, "this might mean something."

He was holding what looked like an old, very well-used zippered plastic bag filled with the pop tops from soda cans.

I shook my head to indicate I wasn't following him. "What am I looking at?"

"Do you know of Gray Dove?" he asked.

"Gray Dove?" I repeated to make sure I'd heard him correctly. "It sounds familiar, but I can't place it."

"He's one of those outsider artists," the officer explained. "One of the most famous in the city. He goes around taking trash and discarded items, transforming them into art pieces and leaving them for people to find. He was part of a big installation in the park a few years back, and he was approached by a couple of galleries about having an actual show to sell his pieces and taking commissions. He flat-out refused. Wouldn't even listen to their offers.

"He said his art was created by what he found. He didn't do it for money. He did it for the items that had been discarded and the people who would see them given another chance and might think differently about what they had in their lives. After that, he wouldn't participate in any larger collectives or anything because he was afraid it was devaluing the purpose of his work."

"What does that have to do with pop tops in a bag?" I asked.

"This is one of his signature mediums. Whenever he finds cans, he immediately takes off the top and puts it in a bag. They become fish scales, feathers on birds, even chain mail. It's incredible what he can do with them. Anyway, the point is, I found this over by the corner of the building leading into the back alley. He would never leave them like that. They're too important to him for him to just drop them and not realize it. And his whole thing is not wasting anything and not disrespecting the environment and the city with trash. He wouldn't just leave them there."

"You said he gave discarded things another chance?" I asked.

He nodded. "That was how he put it."

I looked at Jackson, who had come up beside me and was eyeing the pop tops in my hand. He met my eyes.

"Another chance," he said. "Like new life."

We were both thinking the same thing. The *Frankenstein* clue had brought us here, and it was starting to take on more meaning.

"We need to spread out. Focus right here, then move out in a controlled radius. We need to find Gray Dove." I looked at the officer again. "What else do you know about him? Can you identify places where he might be or where people who know him might be? Where does he live?"

"He's transient by choice," he said.

"So he could be anywhere," I said. I looked around, trying to take in the entirety of the city. There was nothing to do but look. "Let's go."

We searched through the night, plying ourselves with hot coffee to stay awake and warm up our bodies. Finally, when the first streaks of light were starting to show in the sky, I got notice that the artist had been found.

CHAPTER SIXTEEN

I STOOD NEXT TO THE METAL SLAB WITH THE MEDICAL EXAMINER looking down on Gray Dove's face. He looked almost serene, which was somewhat comforting. The way Officer Lautner described him gave the impression of a peaceful, loving man who wanted to make a positive contribution to the world around him, even if he chose to live a life that was unacceptable by most people's standards.

The quiet expression on his face that could almost give the impression of him meditating or sleeping was marred by the trickle of blood frozen to his skin from an open wound on the side of his head.

"I'm obviously going to need to do a full examination to know for sure, but I would guess that blow is the cause of death," Dr. Jess Casey told me. "It looks like he, quite literally, didn't know what hit him."

"So there wasn't a massive struggle? He wasn't running away or trying to fight back?" I asked.

"It doesn't look like it. There aren't any defensive wounds on his hands or other significant abrasions on his body, and the intensity of that impact on his skull would have at the very least rendered him unconscious instantly."

I nodded. "And then he bled out in a dumpster. But at least he didn't suffer, and he wasn't afraid."

The bitter irony of where the artist's body was found wasn't lost on me. There was no way that was unintentional. Neither of the other victims was found discarded like that. Warren Mason was discovered in his own house. Danielle was in an alley. Both appeared to be left in the location where they were murdered. Yet this man had been transported, even for a short distance, to be tossed into a dumpster. The fact that he was known for crafting his art utilizing trash couldn't have been a coincidence.

After talking with the medical examiner, I went back to the police department to start piecing Gray Dove's death into the larger investigation.

"Have you slept at all?" Detective Tarrant asked when she came into the room where I was trying to research the artist.

"No," I told her.

"You need to go get some rest," she said.

"I can't. There's too much to do. While I was investigating the first two murders, someone else was killed. I can't take more time. I can't risk any other lives," I said.

"I understand that, but you know as well as I do you won't be any good if you don't get enough sleep. You're not going to be able to think clearly, and you're going to make mistakes. Go to the barracks. It isn't safe for you to get behind the wheel. And this way you are already right here when you wake up, so you can get right back to it. I'll send a team to find as much information as possible about the victim."

I wanted to protest more, but I knew she was right. As frustrating as it was to have to stop, I knew all too well the potential dangers of sleep deprivation in my line of work. Exhaustion was dragging on me, and the constant stream of coffee was no longer having an effect. I needed at least a couple of hours of rest before I kept going.

Reluctantly leaving my notes behind, I let the detective bring me back to the rooms set up for officers and detectives to catch sleep when they could during intense investigations. She promised to check on me later and closed the door behind her. I kicked off my shoes and climbed under the covers of the cot. As soon as I turned off the lights, I was asleep.

A few hours later, I was back in the conference room. It was far from a full night of rest, but it was enough to refresh me and get me going again.

"Did you get any sleep?" I asked Detective Tarrant when I walked in and found her sitting at the conference table with two officers.

"I was actually asleep when they called me about the books," she said. "I'm getting ready to go home for a while. This is Officer Bryan Morehouse and Officer Chelsea Strong. They can fill you in on what we've found."

"Thank you," I said.

She nodded as she got up and headed for the door. "Give me a call if you need me. I'll be back later this afternoon."

She left the room, and I took the seat she'd vacated. "What do we have?"

"Unfortunately, not much," Officer Morehouse said. "At least not in terms of his personal details. He didn't have any government identification. No one even knows his full legal name, when he was born, where he was from. Anything. We've been trying to trace back mentions of him and his art as far back as we can to see if we can create a timeline of his life that might help narrow those details down."

"Good," I said. "You said you hadn't found much in terms of his personal details. Does that mean you found something else?"

"We did," Officer Strong said. "But it isn't great. He is on record as having a few arrests and spending some time in jail."

"On what charges?" I asked.

"Theft mostly," she said. "A few other minor charges like demonstrating without a permit and trespassing. Nothing serious or violent."

"That tracks with what I've heard about him," I said. "Were you able to find any links to the other two victims? Anything that might suggest they knew each other or had crossed paths?"

"Not so far," Officer Morehouse said. "We've been trying to find a time when they might have overlapped in jail time, but neither of the other two victims have ever spent time in jail other than a couple of stints in the drunk tank for Warren Mason. As far as we can tell, those weren't at the same time as any of Gray Dove's jail stints."

"It's a start," I said.

I was trying to be positive, but at the back of my mind, I felt stuck. I was starting to question whether I was understanding the clues at all. Maybe I was thinking too hard about them and overlooking their actual meaning. By the time Gray Dove was discovered, he had already been dead for two days. The cold weather suppressing the smell of decomposition and the dumpster where he was found being located behind a closed business meant he had gone unnoticed. I hated that. I hated that he was murdered while I was actively investigating, and I hated that a life spent dedicated to making the world more beautiful was snuffed out without anyone even realizing it. He deserved better than that.

Jackson had gone home soon after the discovery of the body, but while I was asleep, he called to tell me he was going down into the city to canvas the homeless community to find out if any of them knew anything. He hadn't come back to the station when I got a message from Stephanie Campano.

"Shit," I muttered.

"It's just some plain English breakfast tea, but I didn't think it was that bad," Officer Strong said, putting a cup down in front of me.

"No," I said, shaking my head. "I just got a message from the English professor up at the school. The one the students were trying to intimidate into leaving campus. She says she's been informally suspended."

"What does that mean?" she asked.

I got up, throwing my coat on and grabbing the cup for a swig of the hot tea. It hadn't steeped all the way yet, and I cringed a little as it went down.

"Yeah, that probably wasn't delicious," she said.

"It was not. But I appreciate it. I think it means the administration asked her not to come to campus while this situation is unfolding. I'm going to talk to her and find out exactly what's going on. I'll have my phone on. Call if anything else comes up."

Stephanie Campano lived in one of the old houses lined up tightly together on a side street not far from campus. She was wearing black leggings and an oversized white fleece sweater when she opened the door, her hair tied up in a messy bun and her hands wrapped tightly around a mug like it was the only thing she felt like she could have a grip on. She sighed heavily when she saw me and walked back into the house without inviting me in.

I stepped inside and shut the door behind me. Noticing a rack in the entryway, I took off my shoes and added my coat to the knobs screwed into the wall. I found Stephanie in the kitchen pouring hot water into a soup mug. Two tea bags hung over the side. She took a spoon from a drawer and handed both to me.

"You strike me as a tea drinker," she said.

I gave her a questioning look. "Is that a particular skill of the literature field I didn't know about?"

"Maybe," she said with a slight chuckle. "Us literature professors do spend a good amount of time sitting around drinking hot beverages and discussing stuffy writers." The brief moment of levity disappeared almost as quickly as it appeared. "Maybe I shouldn't joke about that. That's what got me into this disaster."

"What happened?" I asked. "Did they actually tell you that you're suspended?"

"Not officially. What they said was that in light of the situation, they felt it would be best for everyone involved if I took some time off. I could consider it a sabbatical. Essentially, they are very aware people are linking me to the crimes and are fully convinced I'm responsible, especially now that there's been a third murder. But they don't have any real evidence or reason to think I would do it, and I haven't been arrested, so they can't formally suspend or fire me. All they can do is get my courses covered by a teaching assistant who can follow my syllabus and ask me to stay home so that the students don't completely freak out and start rioting," she told me.

She walked past me into the living room, and I followed her. We sat down, and I took out the small notepad I brought with me. I knew I couldn't tell her what the passages said, but I hoped I could get some input from her about why someone would choose to use literature passages and what kind of connection they might have.

Without telling her the exact passages that had been taken out of each of the books, I gave her the names of the writers and asked if she could think of any way those writers were connected to one another. Stephanie thought about them for a few moments then asked me to repeat the list. I wrote them down for her and handed her the sheet of paper.

She read over them and shook her head. "These don't really make sense in any kind of categorization I can think of. They're all from different times and literary styles. They wrote different things for different audiences and had widely varying impacts."

"So do you think it's safe for me to operate on the understanding that it's not the writers or the books themselves that actually matter but the exact words? Like these don't follow a particular order or any kind of influence that would produce a logical progression of one to the other?" I asked.

"I can't think of any," she said.

"How about details about those writers as people? Things about their lives or what they were known for that might make the victims make sense? Do any of those writers make you think of anything about any of the three victims? I know you weren't familiar with Warren Mason, but you did know Danielle. And you know of Gray Dove, the artist whose body was just found. Is there anything about those writers, their careers, relationships, anything that would connect with any of the victims?" I asked. "I'm sorry I'm having to be so vague, and I know I'm not giving a lot of information for you to go on."

"It's okay," Stephanie said. "I understand you have to keep things confidential. Actually, giving me fewer parameters is helpful. But even thinking about it that way, none of these writers really seem connected to the victims in any particular way. I mean, if we want to stretch a bit, we could say that Mary Shelley and Danielle are connected in both being young women. But she also isn't the only woman on this list.

"On that same token though, you could say that she and the artist have the similarity of both being considered outsiders in a way. Mary Shelley wrote one of the most horrifying stories in literary history at a time when that was way out of line for women. I think any connection that was made would be a leap. It would be stretching to make the connection fit rather than it being genuine in any way. I'm sorry I couldn't help more."

"That's all right. The fact that you could give me that actually is helpful. It validates that I should be focused on the words, not making it more complicated by trying to think beyond that. I'm sorry you're having to deal with being wrapped up in this. I don't know if it's any real comfort or if it will just make you feel worse, but people don't know how to react in situations like this. It's one of those things that they know happen out in the real world. But to other people. It's abstract. When it happens so close to home and affects people they know, it's completely different. The instinct is to try to make it make sense. They want answers as quickly as they can find them so that the world doesn't seem so out of control.

"Jumping to the explanation that you had to have something to do with it because of your affinity for literature is just a way for them to clamp down on that control. It makes them feel better to think that they've seen through lies. If they can pinpoint who did it, that means they haven't been deceived and so they're safe. They can't be a victim if they already know whom to look out for. It isn't personal," I said.

"I know," Stephanie said. "But honestly, that doesn't really help. It doesn't change the way they're looking at me or the things they're saying about me. I had absolutely nothing to do with this, and yet my life is in shambles. No matter what, it's never going to be the same after this. People will always look at me like that. There will always be whispers."

"I know," I said. "I'm sorry. But I'm doing everything I can to bring this to a close as quickly as possible and make sure everyone knows who is actually responsible for these murders."

"Thank you," she said. "And thank you for coming by."

"Of course. You can get in touch with me whenever. If you think there's something I need to know, if something pops into your head, or you just want to have another cup of tea and talk about something other than stuffy writers, don't hesitate to call me."

I left Stephanie's apartment and was going to head for the bookstore to talk with the owners, but a phone call stopped me. It was Tanis, telling me she found another picture of Danielle up on the wall, and she thought I might want to see it.

Back at the coffee shop, Tanis had the picture behind the counter. She handed it over to me, and the back of my neck tingled.

"I just noticed it when I was putting some new sketches up. I don't know the guy personally, but I think I've seen him in here a couple of times. I don't really know for sure. I just thought maybe you'd be able to figure out who he is and track him down. He might not know anything, but he might."

She was still talking, but I'd mostly blocked her out. I was too absorbed in the picture, too lost in the cloudy thoughts building up in my mind. Tanis might not have known the man personally, but I certainly did.

"Thank you," I said. "I appreciate this. If you notice any other ones, let me know."

"Definitely. Can I get you a drink before you go? I know it's cold out there," she said.

"No, I'm good. But thank you. I'm sure I'll see you again soon."

I brought the picture with me outside, and when I was out of sight of the people watching me through the window, I took out my phone.

"We need to talk," I said to the voicemail prompt, which infuriated me when it answered. "Call me back."

I was getting into my car when my phone rang. It was Monique Tarrant.

"Hey," I said. "Did you get some sleep?"

"I did," she said. "Are you near campus?"

"Yeah, I'm at the coffee shop. I'm actually just leaving. Why?"

"A friend of mine who works security at the university just called me. He overheard the dean talking about an emergency meeting being held at the university to discuss the situation and how they are going to handle it moving forward."

"Handle it moving forward?" I asked. "What does that mean?"

"I'm not sure, but you might want to get over there and find out."

"I'm on my way," I said.

CHAPTER SEVENTEEN

I caught sight of Laurie Harrison hurrying across the street as I drove back to campus and rolled my window down to call out to him. He heard me and rushed over to talk to me at the corner where I paused.

"Did you hear about an emergency meeting?" I asked.

"Yes," he said. "That's where I'm headed right now."

"What's it about? I asked. "All I heard was that the administration wants to discuss how the school is going to move forward in light of this situation. I can only imagine that's referring to the murders."

"There have apparently been a lot of complaints and concerned communication about the danger on the campus and nothing being done to address it. The administration wants to open up a forum to talk about possibilities. I think it's something you should hear," he said.

"I do too," I said. "Give me just a second, and I'll park and walk with you."

The massive lecture hall usually used for large classes was already teeming with people when Laurie and I got inside.

"I don't want to be too intrusive," I said. "I think I'm just going to linger back here and listen."

"I am too," he said. "I don't know what's going to be said, and I don't particularly want to be caught up in the middle of a big crowd if things go sideways, if you know what I mean."

We settled into seats in the back section, and within a few moments, the dean walked out onto the small platform stage in front of the hall and up to the podium. She cleared her throat and held up both her hands to get everyone's attention.

"I want to thank everyone for coming out on such short notice. I think this is a very important conversation. I want as many voices heard as possible. If we could please settle in so we can get started," she said.

It took another few seconds of shifting around and reorganizing for everyone to take their seats and stop muttering among themselves.

"Thank you. I'm going to start by acknowledging the difficult times we're all facing. This isn't something any of us prepared for this semester, or anytime really. I commend all of you for your commitment to the school, to the students, and to yourselves as we navigate it. I urge all of you to be aware of your emotions and your mental health and regularly check in to see how you are coping with this situation. We are working to provide access to mental health professionals and other resources for those feeling the need to talk through what they are experiencing or those who feel they have become overwhelmed by the situation. Even if you do not choose to take advantage of these resources, please take care of yourselves and offer support to others.

"With that being said, I want to go right into the purpose of tonight's meeting. As I'm sure all of you are aware by now, a third body was found early this morning. The news has reported that it is linked to the first two. This means that despite our hopes that the loss of the first two victims, including one of our own students, was an isolated incident, the killer is still active.

"Up until now it has been our decision to carry on, continuing classes and allowing students to move around campus freely. But especially with the discovery of another murder, many concerned parents, faculty, and students alike have called for a more proactive response from the school. The purpose of this meeting is to discuss the possibility of canceling further classes and activities, locking down the campus, and requesting all students with the ability to relocate to leave campus until the situation is resolved."

The audience erupted in loud, overlapping responses. The dean held up her hands again to quiet them.

"I know there are strong feelings about this from both sides, which is why we came together to discuss it. I'd like to open the floor to commentary and debate, but I ask that you all show restraint and respect so we can manage this critical conversation efficiently and effectively."

A man in khakis and a light-blue button-down shirt carried a mic stand out in front of the podium and placed it at the end of the main aisle. Immediately, people streamed out of their seats and formed a line that came nearly to the back of the hall.

The first person to step up to the microphone was a woman with silver-gray hair swept into a bun and a black sweater that contrasted with an eclectically patterned skirt down to her knees.

"I sent one of what sounds like many emails the administration has received about this situation. I have to say, I am extremely concerned. I believe in light of the continued threat, the plan to close campus should move forward tonight."

She stepped aside and allowed the next person in line, a younger man in a thick university hoodie camera to approach the microphone.

"I agree. I think it's pretty ridiculous that nothing has been done up until now. It's far too dangerous to just keep going and pretend nothing's happening. The administration is being irresponsible by continuing to have students on campus while this is going on. We are having to choose between feeling safe and going to class. We can't just skip classes until everything's okay, because then we'll fail. That isn't fair for anyone."

"That isn't entirely true," the man behind him said. "There are teachers who are making special accommodations for students who don't feel comfortable coming into class, especially those with night courses."

"Some teachers aren't all teachers," the younger man argued. "It's great for those students to be able to make the decision to stay home, but not all of us get that. My teachers are still taking attendance at every class and requiring assignments to be turned in. I can't afford to get marked down because I don't come to class or finish my work. Shutting everything down will force those teachers to allow everybody to stay safe."

"It will also completely screw up the semester," the woman behind them shouted so she could be heard.

"Can you come up to the microphone so that everyone can hear what you have to say?" the dean asked, gesturing for the woman to step forward.

The others moved to the side so she could access the microphone.

"I understand what people are saying about feeling safe, but we can't just compromise the progress of the entire semester for this. This killer is not targeting our students directly. Two of the three victims have *not* been students on campus. They weren't even found on campus, just in the surrounding city. And the clues were found in several locations, not just in the library. Not to be morbid, but Richmond is a city of more than two hundred thousand people. There are murders in this city all the time. We barely even blink an eye, much less start talking about shutting down classes because of it."

She stepped out of the way to allow the next person to come up behind her.

"That's true," he said. "But also, we don't want to give this killer more power by disrupting everybody's lives because of him. Completely throwing off the academic year and making it difficult, if not impossible, for students who are trying to fulfill their academic requirements isn't going to do anything but make him feel stronger and more important."

I felt Laurie shift beside me and looked over to see him get up. He joined the line of people wanting to speak, and a few moments later, Asher Vance stepped up behind him. The two men noticed each other and shook hands. I couldn't help but feel a twinge of distaste toward Asher for so openly gossiping about the other teacher behind his back, only to be friendly to his face. But at the same time, he hadn't actually said anything mean or judgmental about Laurie, or even about his relationship with Danielle. He'd just acknowledged it, and to his credit, he thought I already knew about it. In a way, maybe he believed he was being helpful with the investigation.

Opinions seemed fairly split as the commentary went back and forth with the people who approached the microphone. Both sides had passionate supporters, and it was difficult to decide how I thought the administration would lean by the end of it. Finally, Laurie had his turn at the microphone. I wondered if he was nervous standing there in front of so many people with the full knowledge that many of them were aware of his relationship with Danielle.

If he was feeling anxious, he didn't show it, and it didn't come out in his voice. Instead, he sounded calm and articulate.

"It would be ridiculous to pretend this situation has not had a significant and tangible effect on our entire community. People are afraid. People are angry. And rightfully so. Lives have been stolen, and the sense of comfort and security we had on our campus has been damaged. I know this isn't by far the first crime that has happened here. And there are many who would argue that they never fully felt safe here. But there's a difference between knowing something could happen and has happened in the past and having to come face-to-face with it. Being forced to go through this is life-changing. No one on this campus or in the surrounding city will ever truly be the same.

"But it's because of that horrific impact that I believe it would be detrimental to close down the campus. Rather than just hiding out and waiting for the danger to end, we should be providing support and encouragement. Everyone here on campus needs to be surrounded by community now. We need as much normalcy and predictability as we can possibly have. With everything around us disrupted and changed, having things we can depend on, even if it is just getting a favorite bagel at the commons before class or sitting at the Compass reading in between classes, is crucial to not just getting through this but healing and moving forward. We should stay open. Perhaps with modifications. But open," he said.

Asher came up behind him and clamped a supportive hand on his shoulder. He looked around, waiting for the spattering of applause that had broken out across the crowd to die down. When it was quiet, he leaned toward the microphone.

"I couldn't agree more with my colleague. Right now is a time to come together and stand strong. And I do believe one-hundred-percent that this experience could be life-changing for our students. In more ways than one. For those of you who don't know who I am, I'm Professor Asher Vance. Among others, I teach a class on criminal psychology and psychology of law enforcement. My students were affected on a very personal level by this case and latched on to it as an opportunity to further their learning and empower themselves in the face of unimaginable adversity.

"They took the reins of the class and have been deeply exploring these murders as the case unfolds. Participating in a mock investigation has encouraged them to think critically and use the skills and knowledge they've acquired throughout their education to attempt to understand the killer and perhaps identify down. Not only has this been an incredibly enriching exercise for them from an academic perspective, but they have also expressed to me that they feel more in control and less afraid because they've been able to talk about it and break it down into its elements rather than just leaving it as the boogeyman waiting for them in the shadows.

"In both ways, this has been a formative experience for them, and it would be an insult to them and to all the work they've done, and the courage they've shown, if you stop them now. We should absolutely give accommodations to anyone needing them. Offer the opportunity to do online classes or makeup work if they need to. Change night classes to day options, or open up meeting spaces in more public areas for those classes that usually meet in the older buildings at the back of campus. But give these students the respect of letting them have the choice," he said.

"That was a moving speech, Mr. Vance," the dean said. "But I have to admit I am a bit taken aback to hear about what sounds like a tremendous deviation from the approved syllabus for your course."

"It was a spontaneous decision made to fulfill the interests of my students. This is exactly why they are in the course of study they are in, and they felt like it was the perfect opportunity to learn in a truly immersive and firsthand way they wouldn't otherwise have the chance to," Vance said.

"I know it's an unconventional approach, but I have to say, I'm really impressed by how Asher is handling this situation with his students. Like he said, this is why they are in school, and he's taking advantage of an opportunity most students, thankfully so, won't ever get. I've heard some of the students talk about the class, and it's all been very positive," Laurie added.

"Thank you," Asher said. "I've been really pleased with how the class has gone, and I've had many students approach me to ask if I'm going to develop it into a seminar. It's something I am definitely considering. I believe this is a chance to create engaging new course options that offer highly focused deep dives into cases specifically within the city. There can be heavily academic versions but also more recreational types to accommodate the interests of those students who are in different courses of study but are still interested in crime and understanding it."

This declaration didn't sit well. In an instant, the meeting went from intense to heated. Students sitting in the audience started shouting, accusing people from both sides of either infantilizing them and overdramatizing a situation, or willfully putting them at risk. Some lashed out against the teachers for what they felt was them unjustly holding their grades hostage when they didn't feel comfortable going to class. Others fought back against them, insisting people were using the murders as an excuse to not do their work.

As the tension ratcheted higher, the dean tried to get it back under her control. She shouted from the podium and waved her arms, but it did little good. No one in the room seemed to be listening to her. I got up and grabbed the bag I'd put by my feet. Pushing through the people now clogging the aisle in an effort to either get to the microphone or stop someone else from getting there, I tried to make my way to the stage. A different voice might catch at least some people's attention and calm things down.

To one side, a group of students suddenly broke into a scuffle. They tumbled up and over the seats, forcing several people in the crowd to fall back a few steps. They crashed into me, and my bag fell from my hands onto the floor. Papers and notes scattered in the space between two rows of seats that had fortunately been largely abandoned by their occupants. As I gathered them, somebody held a handful out to me.

"Thanks," I said. I glanced up and recognized Asher Vance's assistant. "Marcus, right?"

"Yeah. Are you all right? This is getting a little crazy," he said.

I smiled. "I have seen much crazier, but thank you. I was just trying to get up to the podium and see if I could calm everybody down."

"Well, it looks like the people causing the most trouble have already been escorted out, but it couldn't hurt to have somebody get some control over this." He realized he was holding more of my papers. "Oh. Here you go."

"Thanks."

I jogged up to the stage and hopped onto it, dropping my bag onto the floor beside the podium. It wasn't easy wrangling the meeting back into some semblance of order, but I finally managed to get the attendees back into their seats so the conversation could continue. Several people had been ejected and were warned the police would be called if there was any more trouble.

What seemed to finally push the decision was a commentary from the head of security on campus assuring a stronger presence and encouraging people to stay together, share rides, and know where their friends were. The meeting ended with the determination that the university would remain open, operating as it had, but with increased police and security presence, stronger protocols, and statements issued to all faculty encouraging more flexibility and adaptability.

As I expected it to be, the reaction was mixed. It seemed more people than not were either happy or simply resigned to the decision, but those who weren't made their discomfort and anger known. But at that point, it didn't matter. The entire meeting had been such a disaster, and it seemed everyone involved just wanted it to be over with. The decision was nonnegotiable, and everyone in attendance was promptly dismissed.

As I was leaving, I overheard some muttering among the faculty that caught my attention.

"I don't even understand what he is doing here," one teacher said.

"Neither do I. It's so strange."

"Who does he think he is?" a third asked in a scathing whisper. "He really is delusional."

I didn't know who they were talking about, but I was intrigued by the remarks. The women laughed, and I headed back to my car, texting Jackson as I went.

CHAPTER EIGHTEEN

When I got home, I tossed my bag onto the sofa and went for a shower. I stood under the hot water for far longer than I needed to, letting the high pressure and steaming temperature sting on my skin and beat down on my muscles until my shoulders started to relax and the tension from the meeting started to ease. I finally dragged myself out of the shower and put on my favorite sweatsuit and slipper socks. These were the kind of nights I didn't miss the thick hair I used to have hanging down over the back of my neck. Wet hair on your back on a cold night is a miserable feeling I did not long for.

With a massive bowl of heavily buttered popcorn and tea in a chipped vintage FBI mug I found at a thrift store and couldn't resist, I went back to the living room. I intended to sit down and relax for a while, but my eyes kept drifting back over to my bag in the opposite corner of the sofa. I knew all the notes and paperwork inside were in complete disarray after being dropped, and I just couldn't deal with not getting it back in order. I knew the next day when I went to review my notes, I would be furious with past Callan for not straightening them back up.

As a compromise, I pulled up a streaming network and put on my favorite show so I could at least have something entertaining going on in the background while I sorted through everything. I was surprised they weren't more mixed up and messier than they were, but I still took the time to go through each piece and make sure I had everything in the right order. I had just paper-clipped the new picture of Danielle back to the stack of notes specifically about her when I realized one of the papers sitting on the coffee table in front of me didn't belong there.

I set down Danielle's file and picked up the piece of unlined paper. There was a quote written in the center.

Who controls the past, controls the future. Who controls the present, controls the past.

—George Orwell, *Nineteen Eighty-Four*

The words felt like a threat, but at the same time, this was the only time the words had been handwritten on paper rather than taken from or found in a book. It seemed odd and out of place, but still a bit chilling. I didn't recognize the handwriting, and there was nothing on the paper to indicate who wrote it. I dug through the rest of the papers again but didn't find anything else out of place.

It was hard to shake the feeling that came from the paper as I tried to unwind for the rest of the evening, and it was still running down my spine the next morning as I made my way to the library. I wanted to check any copies of the George Orwell book the library had in stock. I had already reached out to the owners of the used-books bookstores to have them do the same.

My phone rang as I approached the library, and I saw it was Jackson. My jaw set, I took a second to take a breath before answering.

"Hey, I got your call and text last night," he said. "Sorry you couldn't get in touch with me. I must have had my ringer off. I heard about the meeting."

"We need to talk," I said, repeating the voicemail I left him the day before after leaving the coffee shop.

"Yeah, you said that. What's going on? Did you find something?"

"Meet me in the study room," I said.

"I'm stopping to grab some coffee. Can I get you anything?" he asked.

"No. Just get here."

I hung up before he said anything else. The review of all the books in the library was finished, so there weren't any officers to check in with before going to the study room. I was agitated and angry. I knew partnership in a case didn't mean we needed to be glued at the hip or always involved in the same aspects of the investigation. Especially considering I was lead on the case, there were things I would be doing on my own, and I wanted that way. But I still found it annoying that I was always chasing Jackson. And now I was fighting suspicions building up in my thoughts.

The picture from the coffee shop was already sitting on the table when he arrived fifteen minutes later. He didn't seem to notice it at first, then he stopped, his eyes locked on the image of him sitting at the counter with Danielle.

"Where did you get that?" he finally asked.

"I have a friend who works at the coffee shop where Danielle did. She found it on the same art wall where I found the picture of Danielle and Warren together. You want to explain that to me?" I asked.

"I wasn't sure it was her," he said.

I rolled my eyes. "Don't give me that."

"No, seriously," he said. "When you found out she worked in that coffee shop, I didn't even think about it at first. Then I realized it was the same one I went to quite a bit when I was handling another case. But that was months ago. Almost a year. She and I chatted when I would come in. I asked her on a date. She rejected me. And that was the end of that. The case wrapped up, and I didn't go there much anymore. I hadn't really put much thought into it, and I wasn't even positive it was her."

"You carried on conversations with this girl and thought enough of her to ask her on a date, but you couldn't remember her name or recognize her when you found out she had been murdered?" I asked.

"Like I said, it was months ago, and I only went in over the course of a couple of weeks, maybe. I don't really date a lot. I thought she was cute, so I took a leap. It didn't work out for me, and I moved on. Somebody took a picture of us while I was hanging out there one day. They took pictures of a lot of people. It's not like we're hanging on each other or kissing or anything. We're just talking," he said.

"Is there anything else you need to tell me?" I asked. "Anything you've been keeping from me because you didn't think it was a big deal or you just conveniently didn't remember?"

"I didn't conveniently not remember," he said through gritted teeth.

"Anything, Jackson? Do you have anything you need to tell me?"

He stared at me with darkened eyes for a few moments, his jaw working back and forth slightly beneath his skin. His shoulders dropped, and a resigned expression crossed his eyes.

"Before I went to the Academy and joined the FBI, I was a police officer here," he said. "After Gray Dove was found, I thought he seemed familiar, and I looked him up. A year before I left the force, he was involved in a situation, and I arrested him."

I squeezed my eyes shut. "For what?"

"Assault on an officer."

"Shit," I said. "Damn it, Jackson. Are you serious right now?"

"It was years ago," he protested. "And obviously it got resolved because it isn't even recorded in his file that there was an assault. Like you already found out, his record doesn't show anything violent. The only reason I knew it was him was that I recognized the location and remember the incident well. It was a protest at an empty lot. Residents in the neighborhood around it had been using it as a little pocket park, but a developer bought it and planned to build on it. It's listed on his record as 'Demonstrating without a permit' and 'Mischief.'"

"Do you have any idea how bad this looks? Any idea at all?" I asked.

He looked at me incredulously. "You think I could have done this?"

"I haven't been able to get ahold of you several times. You haven't been involved in important parts of the investigation. Your behavior has been erratic. And now I know you have a personal connection to all three victims," I pointed out.

Jackson's mouth fell open slightly, and he blinked a few times. "I thought we had found some common ground the other night. I thought maybe this was going to work out. Now I know my partner thinks I'm a serial killer." He shrugged back into the coat he'd draped over one of the chairs and grabbed his drink. "Thanks."

"Where are you going?"

"I have some more people to talk to," he said.

I watched him leave with a burning feeling deep in my gut. It was impossible not to feel uneasy considering the facts, but I was also reluctant to fully believe something so awful as my partner being responsible for these crimes. Just looking at the details that had come to the surface, it seemed like that was where this was leading. But that in and of itself gave me pause. The signs pointed at Jackson almost too conveniently. It was hard to fathom him having a connection to each of the three victims coincidentally, yet this was a former police officer and current special agent of the FBI. It felt extremely unlikely he would not have put more effort into hiding those connections with the victims if he had been involved. The entire situation was strange and left me feeling off-balance for the rest of the morning.

THE GIRL AND THE SECRET PASSAGE

A call from an unidentified number came as I was walking out to the entrance of the library to pick up my lunch from the delivery driver. If it was my personal phone, I likely wouldn't have answered the call, but my work number was distributed to people related to my investigations who needed to get in touch with me, so I hit the button and tucked the phone between my ear and shoulder.

"Thorne," I said as I reached out to accept my bag and sign the card receipt.

"This is Barbara Scherer," a woman's voice said. "Danielle Scherer's mother."

"Oh. Hello, Mrs. Scherer. How can I help you?"

"I've already been in touch with Detective Tarrant and the university, but they said I needed to speak with you as well. I would like to have Danielle's things sent to me," she said.

"Sent to you?" I asked, walking back into the library and heading for the study room.

"Yes. You have permission to use whatever you need as evidence provided there is a clear record kept and those things are also returned to us as soon as possible."

"I thought you would be coming into town to collect her belongings," I said.

Not to mention her body.

"Our plans had to be changed. We won't be coming to the city to retrieve anything and won't be further involved in the investigation."

CHAPTER NINETEEN

I was so stunned I stood with the phone in my hand for several seconds after Barbara Scherer hung up. When I could get my brain operating again, I called Nathan.

"Hey, it's Callan Thorne," I said when he answered. "Do you have a second?"

"Sure," he said.

I sat down and spread my lunch out on the side of the table I hadn't covered with my work.

"I just had a very strange conversation with Barbara Scherer. She's trying to make arrangements to have all of Danielle's things sent to her rather than coming to get them. She's also refusing to come to the city or continue to cooperate with the investigation," I said.

At that point Danielle's body hadn't been released and was still in the morgue pending further examination and testing, but I didn't mention that to Nathan. He knew she hadn't been able to have a funeral yet and was aware she hadn't been buried. I didn't need to compound the grief he was suffering any more than was necessary for the case.

"That sounds like her," he said, surprising me with how unaffected he seemed.

"It does? I asked.

"Yeah. Danielle's relationship with her family was… really strained. She didn't like to talk about it. It really upset her, and she was embarrassed about it. But things weren't good between them. She told me they were never particularly nurturing and that it felt like they were relieved when she left for college because she wouldn't be around much anymore. At the same time, they tried really hard to control her and have her do and be exactly what they wanted. When she wouldn't, it just made things worse. Coming all the way here just to get her belongings isn't something either of her parents would place a lot of value on. It doesn't surprise me at all that they found something to have precedence over their responsibilities to their daughter. She actually called me too," he said.

"Do you know them well?" I asked.

"Danielle and I have been together for years. I've spent time with them. Not much, but neither did she. I definitely wouldn't say I knew them well, but well enough for them to contact me to put me in charge of emptying her apartment. I told her she was going to have to talk to the people in charge of the murder case to make sure it was okay before I did anything. The last thing I want to do is accidentally compromise something or move something when I'm not supposed to. I just got a text from her right before you called saying it's fine," he said. "It is, isn't it?"

"Yes. You cleaning out her apartment and sending everything home is perfectly fine. It's very kind of you. When are you planning on going?" I asked.

"In about two hours," he said.

"Would you mind if I met you there?"

"That's fine," he said.

"Great. I'll see you then."

I finished lunch and made a couple of calls, then I saw it was getting close to the time I was supposed to meet Nathan. I didn't want to start up another task that might make me lose track of time. Instead, I got her address from her file and headed to her apartment building. A sign at the entrance warned that resident or guest parking passes were required to park in any of the marked spots, and when I got fully into the parking lot, I discovered the majority of the spots were marked.

I finally found a small section without markings. A sign there noted it was prohibited to stay in those spots for more than three hours. It seemed the management was trying to create a sense of security and exclusivity in the complex, but all I could think was how anxiety-inducing it had to be for anyone living there.

Parking in one of the unmarked spots, I headed toward the building where Danielle's apartment was. I looked out for Nathan's car as I approached but didn't see it. A sudden movement on my side made me turn my attention toward a sidewalk leading off the main one I was walking on and to the individual buildings. I noticed a young man rushing toward the main sidewalk, his head down as he frantically typed something into his phone. I recognized him as the quiet boy from the crime class who spoke about Danielle as being one of his best friends.

"Hey," I called out.

He stopped and looked up. A flush of color rose to his cheeks, and his eyes went wide. He looked nervous, like he was uncomfortable seeing me there.

"Agent Thorne. Remember me from class?"

He nodded, "Hi."

"I actually didn't catch your name," I said, getting closer.

He shifted around, moving his phone from one hand to the other and looking down at it anxiously.

"John," he said.

"John," I repeated. "Do you live in this complex?"

He stammered for a second. "No, I..."

An alert on his phone seemed to startle him, and as he moved his hand, something fell out of it and onto the ground. He bent down to snatch it up, but before he could put it out of sight again, I could see it was a set of keys. A large decorative key chain spelled out a name in pink metal. *Danielle.*

"Did those keys belong to Danielle Scherer? Why do you have them?" I looked behind him and realized he'd been walking away from Danielle's building when I first noticed him. "Were you in her apartment?"

THE GIRL AND THE SECRET PASSAGE

It didn't seem completely out of the ordinary for people close enough to describe each other as best friends to have spare keys to the other's apartment, but the key ring he was holding had clearly belonged to Danielle. This wasn't a matter of him using a key she gave him to access her apartment like he did on a regular basis. Even that would have been cause for concern. Generally speaking, going into a murder victim's home without notifying the authorities and then being exceptionally nervous when caught wasn't a great look. Not criminal, perhaps, but certainly shady.

"You do realize that stealing somebody's keys and using them to access their home is still considered breaking and entering, even if they're dead," I said.

"Yes," he blurted out. "I was in her apartment. But I wasn't breaking and entering. And I didn't steal her keys."

"Then where did you get that?" I asked.

He looked reluctant to answer that question.

"John?"

I heard the familiar voice coming from behind John, but his sizable stature made it so I couldn't see anyone coming up the sidewalk. He turned around.

"Hey, I got your text. I thought you'd already left," Nathan's voice sounded tense.

John's shoulders tightened as his stance shifted in response to the words.

"She's going to be here..."

John moved a step to the side so I was visible. Nathan's face dropped.

"Hi, Nathan," I said.

"She's here now," he said.

"Is there a problem with that? I told you I'd meet you here," I said.

The two men looked at each other for a long beat.

"What's going on?"

"She thinks I stole Danielle's keys," John said to Nathan. "She's wondering why I was in the apartment and thinks it might have been breaking and entering."

There was a note of something in the words that was close to desperation, like he was pleading with Nathan with a different message.

"Can we go inside?" Nathan asked me.

"Sure. Lead the way," I said.

Nathan went down the sidewalk first, followed by John. I came up behind but stayed close enough that I was sure they weren't whispering to each other. Something was definitely happening, and I needed to find out what it was. I half expected Nathan to take the set of keys out of John's hand and use them to get into the apartment, but instead, he drew his own keys out of his pocket and used those. We stepped inside, and he shut the door behind us.

Even without having known Danielle, stepping into her apartment felt like going back in time a little bit. The scent of her perfume still lingered in the air. Mail she hadn't gotten around to opening sat on the corner of the entryway table. It felt like at any moment, she was just going to walk back in.

"He didn't steal the keys," Nathan said. "I gave them to him. John and I are together."

I looked back and forth between them, processing what he'd just told me.

"You gave your boyfriend's keys to the apartment that used to belong to your long-term girlfriend who was murdered and who—"

"She knew," Nathan said.

"What?"

"She knew," he repeated. "Danielle knew about John and me. And before you start jumping to any conclusions, he and I have been together longer than Danielle and I have. It's actually the only reason for our supposedly perfect relationship."

His voice started to tremble, and tears sparkled in his eyes.

"I can't be honest with my family about John. We had been together for a while when I met Danielle. Things were starting to get serious between us, and Danielle and I got very close. I told her everything. I confided in her that there was a massive conflict with my family, and I couldn't tell them or let them find out. She was the one who suggested that she should be my cover-up.

"She was extremely focused and driven in her education, so getting out and dating just wasn't a priority for her. We were already best friends, spending just about all of our spare time together, so it seemed like the perfect idea. And it has been. For all this time. I loved her. It might not have been the way that people thought, but I loved her."

It was deeply sad, and I found myself aching for the two young men standing in front of me. Especially Nathan. It was so obvious he cared so much for Danielle and had a deep appreciation for what she had done for him. Her loss now took on a different dimension. It wasn't just about her being gone. His entire life had changed, and he had to navigate even more than I thought. This gave me a new perspective on Nathan, but it also eliminated the possible motive of jealousy if he discovered Danielle was cheating on him with Laurie Harrison. Since their relationship wasn't real, she wasn't cheating on him. They were just now acting as each other's cover.

"So why did you have Danielle's keys, John?" I asked.

"I found something, but got scared. I didn't want to get more involved and possibly cause problems. I was trying to fix the situation," he explained.

"What do you mean?" I asked. "What didn't you want to get more involved with?"

"Just before Danielle's death, I borrowed a book from her apartment that I thought I could use for a project. I ended up not even opening it because a different resource came up, but after everything happened, I started flipping through it. I found a torn page. It immediately felt like that had something to do with the case, but I couldn't bring myself to tell anybody. I wanted to try to get the book back into the apartment so it could be discovered when it was being cleared out," John said.

"You suspected that you had evidence in a murder case found in the apartment of one of the victims, and you didn't tell anybody?" I asked incredulously. "You didn't think to call the police or even approach me after you've seen me in the crime class? Or even Professor Vance? You could have told him, but you decided not to say anything."

"I know it was a mistake. I should have told somebody. But I was scared. You don't understand what this feels like," he said.

"It isn't just that Danielle was murdered so now we don't have her to cover our relationship anymore," Nathan said. "She was the closest person to our world. We've both been terrified since it happened. John didn't want either one of us to be associated with that book and possibly make ourselves more of a target. We're already trying to figure out what comes next. It wasn't the right thing to do, but he felt like he had to do it."

I closed my eyes, pressing my fingertips to my temples and taking a few deep breaths. I was upset and angered at the revelation, but at the same time, I understood the compulsion. Being that close to a series of violent murders would already be frightening. When the sanctity of the most closely guarded secret of your life was now teetering on the edge of destruction because of that murder, it took it to another level. Aligning themselves with that book would just shove them into a spotlight neither one of them was ready to take.

"Where's the book?" I asked.

John took a copy of *Gone with the Wind* by Margaret Mitchell off a shelf and brought it over to me. He flipped through it until he found the torn page, then handed it to me.

"I'm not familiar enough with the book to know what that section is supposed to say," he said.

"I need to get my computer from the car," I said. "Danielle's was seized for evidence. I'll be right back."

I jogged back out to the car to get my computer so I could search out the passage from the book. It felt like the brief break gave all of us some much-needed time to breathe. Back inside, I started my search for a copy of the book. This time I was lucky. A virtual copy of that exact edition was available. Comparing several pages showed it was an exact match and the digital version hadn't altered any of the page numbers or layout.

"'Tomorrow I'll think of some way to get him back. After all, tomorrow is another day,'" Nathan read.

"It sounds like that could be referencing your relationship," I pointed out. "Some sort of commentary on the arrangement you all had."

"No," Nathan insisted. "It wasn't like that. It was never like that. There was nothing contentious or negative in our relationship. Ever. This wasn't a situation of Danielle trying to get me to love her or trying to save our relationship. This was the way things were. It was the way they had always been."

"Did anyone else know about your relationship?" I asked.

"No, John said. It was just the three of us."

"I find it really difficult to believe that this could have been going on for years without anybody else in your lives finding out about it," I said. "There weren't any other friends you told? Maybe people who could have accidentally seen you two together and figured something out?"

"No," Nathan said firmly. "This arrangement was how my life kept functioning. We agreed from the very beginning that none of us would ever talk about it. The only time John and I were able to be together the way we wanted to be was when we were completely alone at his place or when we were here with Danielle. No one else ever saw us together. We never had any big blowout fights that would have led to her blurting it out to somebody."

"And she never had anybody special in her life who she might have wanted to be in a relationship with that would have been compromised by this arrangement?" I pointed out.

"You're talking about Laurie," he said.

"You knew about that?" I asked.

"Of course I did," he said. "Remember, she was my best friend. The closeness that everybody saw was real. We talked to each other about everything, including him. That relationship didn't impact ours at all.

If anything, it made her even more committed to our arrangement because now we were covering up for each other. Even though she was no longer his student when she reconnected with him, she knew it didn't look good.

"His reputation was at risk, which could have compromised his career. It could have invalidated all the hard work she had been doing in the eyes of other people at school. She knew they couldn't risk being open about their relationship, but they dearly wanted to be together. So they were. She and I saved each other. But even he didn't know about John and me. There wasn't anyone who would be able to use this as a threat."

"All right," I said. "So we have to think about this from a different angle. John, tell me more about this class with Professor Vance. I know I've sat in on a couple of the sessions, but I want to know about it from the perspective of one of the students. How did it turn into what it is now?"

"It just did," he said. "I know that's not very helpful, but at the beginning of the semester, we were working on a completely different syllabus. Then some of the people in the class started talking about the murders and brought it up a couple of times. Then he decided to go along with it and focus the entire class on the case."

"Was it the same people who kept bringing up wanting to talk about it?" I asked. "Like any one person in particular?

"Anthony and Sydney both talked about it a couple of times, but they weren't the only ones."

I nodded, letting that sink in for a few seconds. "Has anything new come up, anything strange that anybody in class said that might mean something? Either in the class or in discussions outside of it?"

"Not really. There are all kinds of theories and thoughts, but I don't think any of us really have a solid grasp. This is also much more overwhelming than any of us would have expected. Some people in the class still think Professor Campano could have had something to do with it. Other people go back and forth on whether they think it was random. We all agreed the book passages obviously meant something, but then a couple of people turned around on that and said they were just a red herring thrown to confuse people. The conversations can get really confusing sometimes," John said.

"How does the teacher handle it?" I asked. "How does he guide how you see the evidence or how you evaluate it?"

"A lot of times, he doesn't," John said. "He goes over stuff with us and presents us with the new evidence that comes up and answers questions, but like he said from the beginning, he's just there as a facilitator. The point of the class is to allow us to explore and investigate the case kind of on our own."

"Is there anybody in the class who doesn't want to be talking about this case? Or anybody who left the class because of the change in the syllabus?" I asked.

"There are definitely people who don't want to be doing it. But a lot of us wouldn't be in the class if we didn't have to be. It's mandatory for our major, we had to do it," he said.

"Why do you say you wouldn't be in the class if you didn't have to be?" I asked. "I thought this was a class all of you wanted to take for your future careers?"

"It isn't about the class," he said. "It's Vance. Think about when you were in school. Wasn't there one teacher you tried to avoid? Somebody you just didn't like and didn't want to have to sit in a classroom with for an entire semester? That's him."

"So what was this class supposed to be about? What were you supposed to study according to the original syllabus?" I asked.

"It was still the same type of idea, only without the mock investigation element. We were supposed to focus on other cases and what was learned from them. It was a continuation of the class from the semester before. Both portions of the class are required, so even people who were very seriously against the idea of focusing entirely on these murders were reluctant to drop the class because that would mean having to repeat it and really throwing off their entire schedule."

"What kind of cases?" I asked. "Had you started on one in particular?"

"This semester was supposed to focus on famous cases that were going cold despite there being suspects. The intention was to discuss the psychology of the suspects and how that contributed to their crimes as well as how the investigation would affect them and how their individual behaviors and perspectives would ultimately influence the investigation. There was supposed to be an element of what techniques could be used to hopefully make them crack so that they would give confessions. In cases that had multiple suspects, we were supposed to discuss each and determine which we thought was most likely. Even though it wasn't technically supposed to be an investigation, a lot of us thought there was a possibility we could actually help solve some of these cases," he told me.

"That isn't an outlandish thought," I told him. "There are instances of classes or clubs looking into cases and ending up finding the piece of evidence that solves them. It happens."

I let what he told me tumble around in my brain. While I knew the benefits of that type of class and the critical knowledge students could get from it, I also acknowledged the potential risks. They were planning to talk about cases that were currently ongoing, though not as close as the one they ended up focusing on. If the actual perpetrator of one of those cases found out about the class, it could be very upsetting and disruptive to them. That alone could be enough to cause them to lash out. They might even have conjured up the idea of the killings as a way to shut down the school and end the class. It was an extreme reaction, but not one that fell out of line with the also extreme behaviors of serial killers.

But while this could explain an overall motive, it didn't give any more insight into the victims themselves or why they were chosen.

"Do you mind if I search around the apartment some?" I asked. "I know the police already did and said they didn't find anything, but I'd like to look around."

I wasn't really asking for permission, but I wanted to maintain the comfortable, positive rapport we had established. They agreed, offering to help, and we embarked on a thorough search of the space. It was a small apartment, so there wasn't much to look through, and little stood out to me. It looked like any other graduate student's apartment.

In the bedroom, I found a desk that surprised me with how messy it was. Danielle seemed like the type of person who would be meticulously organized, and the rest of the apartment exhibited that. Her desk, however, was covered in books, papers, and various other artifacts of her studies.

"Was this always like this?" I asked, thinking I might have stumbled on an indication of somebody else being in her apartment, possibly looking for that book.

Nathan chuckled softly, ending that conjecture.

"Yeah. That was one of the weird things about her. Everything else in her life was so put together. And she was so focused on school. But her desk was always a complete disaster. No matter what. Even when she decided she was going to try to get it all organized, it was just never neat. It was almost like she put so much of her energy and effort into school itself that she lost all control when it came to her space," he said.

The laughter faded quickly from his eyes as he looked over everything piled up on the surface of the desk.

"I don't even know what I'm supposed to do with all of that. Her mother said to send everything, but I can't imagine that they would care about any of this. Would they want her books? The projects she was working on? Her papers and old blue books? Would any of that mean anything to them?"

"I don't know," I said. "I can't really answer that. But if I had to guess, I would say they wouldn't care. I think they are expecting things like clothes and personal belongings."

I stepped up to the desk and looked over what was on it. I noticed a stack of papers that seemed to be set off from the rest, like it was something she was working on the day of her death. I picked them up and looked over them. Something started to click in the back of my mind, but I wasn't sure exactly what.

"Would you mind if I went to class with you?" I asked John. "There's something I might want to get everybody to talk about."

CHAPTER TWENTY

We had taken longer to go through the apartment than we thought and struggled to find parking, so by the time we made it into the classroom, we were already a few minutes late. Instead of slipping into a lecture already in progress however, we found the other students talking and no sign of Asher Vance.

"Hey," John said. "Where's Vance?"

"Nobody knows," Anthony said. "We've been sitting here waiting for him, and he hasn't shown up."

John took out his phone and looked at it. "Did I miss an email?"

"If he had sent out an email, why would the rest of us be sitting here?" Sydney asked, the acidic snap back in her voice.

"This isn't like him," John said, looking at me. "He doesn't miss class. And the couple of times he ever has, he sent out notice ahead of time and there was a substitute. Or at least Marcus was here. He loved it when he got to take over a class, even just part of it because Vance was going to be late or had to leave early. Most teaching assistants would just kind of throw prepared notes up, but he really taught the class."

"This is really weird," Jeffrey said.

He sounded worried, and looking around at the faces of the rest of the students, I saw it seemed that sentiment was shared.

"You don't think...," one of the students started.

"Don't even say it, Prue," another stopped her.

"Why not?" Anthony asked. "It's what we're all thinking."

They didn't have to elaborate. Considering everything that had happened, I knew exactly what was going through each of their minds. I stepped off to the side and took out my phone. I called Jackson. He didn't answer, and I spoke to the very familiar voicemail box.

"Look, I know you don't want to talk to me, but you really don't have that option right now. Asher Vance is not in class. Nobody has heard from him, and the students can't figure out where he is. I need you to start calling and looking around and trying to locate him," I said. "Get back in touch as soon as you know something."

I ended the call and put my phone back in my pocket.

"What about Marcus? You mentioned he sometimes covers class when Vance isn't here."

"None of us have heard from him either," Jeffrey said.

"Has anybody gone down to his office to see if he might be there?" I asked.

"I walked by on the way to class about half an hour ago," Prue said. "The door was open, but I didn't see anybody inside. I figured he had just stepped out for a second and I'd see him in a couple of minutes."

"You didn't see either of them?" I asked.

"No."

"All right, I'm going to go down to the office to check there. I'd appreciate it if you all waited here until I come back," I said.

I made my way to Asher's office, not sure what to expect. Prue said she'd seen the door standing open with no one inside, but there was no indication of anything being wrong. She didn't seem bothered by the fact that the door was open without seeing anyone, meaning that was something she'd seen before. It didn't necessarily mean there was a problem. Yet in the context of the situation, it didn't seem good.

The door to the office was partially open as I approached, and when I got to it, I could see Marcus sitting at the desk inside, hunched over papers he seemed to be closely scrutinizing. A red pen in his hand flew furiously over the page, and he tossed it to the side onto a stack with a look bordering on disgust. I pushed the door open, and he didn't bother to lift his head.

"Neither of us are available for office hours," he said monotonously. "You will need to come back at another time."

"That really isn't an option since it seems neither of you are available for class either," I said.

His head snapped up, and his cheeks turned pink when he saw me. "Callan. Agent Thorne. I'm sorry, I didn't realize it was you. Students have a habit of just coming in sometimes. It's why I usually don't work with the door open. But the heat seems to be working very well in this room, and it was getting oppressive." He stopped talking, and a questioning look came over his face. "Did you just say neither of us were in class?"

"I did," I said. "The students are waiting in the classroom, but Asher isn't there. They said they didn't get an email or any kind of notification that class wasn't being held today, and that usually if something like that was happening, you would come in to teach."

He frowned. "Well, yes, but he should be there. I spoke with him earlier today to let him know I wouldn't be able to be in class because I have a doctor's appointment that got moved up. He wanted to talk about his lesson plan and make sure that some papers got graded. I told him I had time before my appointment to handle all the administrative tasks. That's why I'm here."

It sounded suspicious. I looked at the desk and noticed several papers arranged around him. My mind went to the unexplained quote I found in my bag after the heated community meeting.

"If you had a doctor's appointment that was stopping you from going to class, why are you still in the office now?" I asked. "Class is supposed to be in session right now, so shouldn't you not be here?"

"There was a miscommunication with the office," he explained. "They had called me to say that my appointment got moved up, but then called again when I was on the way to tell me the doctor actually wasn't coming in today and I would need to reschedule. I didn't want to interrupt by going into class late. He really hates that."

"And you haven't heard anything from him?" I asked.

Marcus shook his head, snatching his phone off the corner of the desk where it sat and looking at it. "I don't have any calls, texts, or emails. The last time I had any communication with him was that call earlier today."

"Did he sound strange at all? Is it normal for you to have calls like that?"

"No, he didn't sound strange in any way. We have calls like that regularly. I'm often responsible for acquiring materials or preparing resources for the students, so if he refines a lesson plan or comes up with an additional activity he wants to do, he lets me know," Marcus told me.

"What about today? What had he come up with for today's class?" I asked.

"He wanted to talk about what influences the start of a series of crimes. He wanted the students to compare the difference between what might motivate a spree killer versus a mass murderer versus a serial killer. And also what might motivate crimes in different contexts."

"What did he mean by that?" I asked.

"He was going back into his original syllabus a bit to compare old cases with this one. To look deeper into what would motivate someone to kill multiple people in a series versus a mass killing in a setting such as a mall or transit station versus a mass killing in a setting such as a house of worship or a demonstration."

"And these were things that were in his former syllabus?" I asked.

"Most of it, yes. He thought it was a good idea to anchor the study of this particular case in relation to others that occurred in the area or nearby," he said.

I looked around the office, taking in the bookshelves, a small table to the side, and a chair in the corner. Files, papers, testing booklets, and books were stacked on nearly every surface. Copies of Asher's published works as well as articles he had written accusing people of certain crimes were prominently displayed on the walls. He was clearly adamant about his views on certain crimes and wasn't afraid to be outspoken about it. It definitely looked like he could have made one of these people very angry or could have enticed a fame-hungry copycat to start acting out so they could get some attention as well.

I examined the articles more closely, taking note of the dates and locations.

"Please try to get in touch with him. Let him know I need to speak with him. If you're available to teach the class, the students are waiting. But I'll warn you, they are agitated. I'd ask you not to get into any conjecture. Either teach the class or dismiss it for the day. I think it would be a better idea if you went down to the classroom and told the students class was canceled for the day. I'd ask that you not elaborate on anything having to do with Asher or the situation."

I left the office and headed out of the building, intending to go to the police station to talk to Detective Tarrant.

THE GIRL AND THE SECRET PASSAGE

As I was walking through the vestibule, I noticed a bulletin board advertising upcoming events and activities. The gears in my mind that had already started turning began clicking into place more rapidly. I pulled the papers I had taken from Danielle's apartment out of my bag and scanned them. I read over the Margaret Mitchell passage again.

"Tomorrow I'll get him back," I whispered. "After all, tomorrow is another day."

Stuffing the papers away again, I jogged out of the building toward my car. I knew exactly what I needed to do.

CHAPTER TWENTY-ONE

Peter Carver almost didn't notice the woman in the water. His early-morning jog along the river was a ritual for him, some time to himself where he could sink into his own thoughts and prepare for the rest of the day ahead. If his wife hadn't uploaded a new playlist to their music account and he hadn't stopped to change the song that came up, he might never have noticed. He would have just kept going, pushing through the last bit of his usual route so he could get out of the cold morning fog.

But he did stop. Still bouncing back and forth to keep his heart rate up and the blood flowing through his legs, he pulled out his phone and made a face at the screen.

"Who listens to this while they're working out, Sandy?" he muttered to himself.

He found his own playlist and got the stronger, faster music going. He put the phone back in the pouch at his hip and twisted at his waist to loosen up the muscle that had been giving him trouble the last couple of days. As his head swiveled toward the dark water moving lazily against the rocky shore, he noticed a flash of color where it should not have been. He leaned closer and saw it was a vibrant green sock sticking out from the cuff of black pants.

He took several steps closer and realized there was a woman floating in the water, one shoulder wedged between rocks that kept her from flowing out further into the river.

Taking off his headphones, he shouted down, "Hey! Are you all right?"

He knew the question was ridiculous even as it was coming out of his mouth. Of course, she wasn't all right. Few people, if any, ever entered the James River at this point during even the hottest days of summer. No one would want to be in it during the harsh chill of early January. And even if some brave, or reckless, soul did decide they were going to get into the polar plunge trend and go for a bracing dip, they wouldn't then linger on the rocks that way. Something was very wrong. But shouting to her was the only thing that came into his mind. Everything else went blank.

When the woman didn't respond or move, Peter's thoughts kicked back in, and he scrambled down from the path to the edge of the water. His instinct was to grab on to the woman and drag her out of the water, but he didn't know if he might hurt her further or end up in the freezing water himself. Instead, he grabbed his phone out of his pocket again and called emergency services.

It felt like hours that he crouched there by the edge of the water holding on to the woman like it would somehow help her. His hands felt frozen, his fingers aching and his skin stinging, but he wouldn't let go until he saw the lights flashing overhead and first responders pulled him away.

Suddenly, the peaceful morning shattered into a frantic rescue. Police and paramedics dislodged the woman's body from the rocks and pulled her up onto the shore. Peter hadn't been able to tell whether she was breathing. He thought she was, but the breaths were so shallow he couldn't really tell if they were her pulling air into her lungs or the movement of the water was creating an illusion. He was relieved when the first paramedic to drop down onto the ground beside her and check her vitals confirmed she had a pause and was breathing.

But she was still in dire condition. They didn't know how long she had spent in the incredibly cold water, and there was evidence of serious injuries all over her body. They couldn't tell what caused those injuries. It was possible she had fallen while walking along the edge of the rocks or perhaps she had jumped from one of the bridges. Either would have caused injury on impact and further damage when she tumbled down the river.

Now that they had confirmed she was alive, they acted quickly to bundle her into an ambulance and rush her to the emergency room.

"Her body temperature is extremely low," the paramedic said as the ambulance barreled down the road. "But the one good thing about that is it helped slow down her blood loss."

"Do we have ID?" his teammate, who was on the phone with the hospital preparing them for arrival, asked.

"Not yet," the first said.

They pulled away her soaked, near-frozen coat and started to cut away her sweater when the man stopped and stared down at her.

"What is it?" the other asked.

"I got ID," the paramedic said, reaching down to lift the lanyard holding an FBI badge up from the woman's chest. "Callan Thorne."

The doctors were still working on her when Eric got the call. He knew in that instant there wasn't going to be a chance Callan would be able to return to her case. He picked up the phone again and made the only call he knew would finish this.

CHAPTER TWENTY-TWO

Emma

Now

I STAND LOOKING OUT OVER THE SPOT WHERE A JOGGER FOUND Agent Callan Thorne partially submerged and caught on rocks. It's unbelievably lucky that he did. According to the doctors, she was very close to death. If he hadn't seen her when he did and made sure she was pulled out of the water, she likely wouldn't have been able to survive the low temperature much longer. I shiver and wrap my coat tighter around myself. It's rainy, gray, and miserable, and looking at the dark water flowing by only seems to make the air feel more raw and biting.

This area perfectly crystallizes the spirit of Richmond. Nearby the city has been given new life with the canal walk and all the activities constantly cropping up around there, from little restaurants and shops to boat tours going up and down a section of the canal. But there are still corners that are remnants of the old city, skeletons of the past. Even just a look down into the water shows chunks of concrete with rusted metal protruding out, fragments of old structures and bridges.

I have many memories of this city, good and bad, and it's those memories that make me feel somehow drawn to Callan. I find myself trying to connect with her, thinking that she at once reminds me so much of myself and is yet so different.

"Agent Griffin?"

I turn around and see Jackson.

"Hi, Jackson," I say. "Thank you for meeting me out here."

"What can I do for you?" he asks.

"I believe Callan was here because of something having to do with the case. I wanted to ask you why she came out here alone. She was obviously doing something dangerous. You should have been here with her."

Jackson gives me a quizzical look. "I don't know. I didn't even know she was here. She didn't tell me she was coming out here or what she was doing. I had no idea until I got the call that she had been injured and was in the hospital. I had a voicemail from her from earlier in the day about Asher Vance…"

"The psychology teacher from the university?" I ask. "The one who's missing?"

"Yes. That's actually what it was about. She had gone to sit in one of his classes, and he hadn't shown up. People were looking for him, and nobody could figure out where he was. So she called me to have me try to track him down. She didn't say what she was going to be doing next. I'm guessing that was coming out here," he tells me.

This strikes me as very odd. Though there is no clear evidence around Callan to indicate why she was down at the river or how she ended up in the water, it seems obvious to me she was investigating something that came up in the case. It was important enough to come down to the river at night and face what turned out to be a treacherous situation. So why didn't she tell her partner? Was there a reason she didn't want him to know what she was doing?

It reminds me so much of myself, but that doesn't seem like a great thing. As much as I have defended the many times I went against protocol and allowed my instinct to push me forward, I don't want to think of this girl doing things so recklessly. From what I have heard about her, Callan has a very strong independent streak and prefers to do things on her own, but she has always shown total understanding of protocol and respect for things as they should be done. She has always been careful to stay safe during investigations, including being connected to other team members. Ending up out here doesn't sound like her.

But I know from my own experience that doesn't mean it wasn't her. It simply means there must have been a very good reason.

"I hear Callan had a room in the university library," I say.

Jackson nods. "There's a study room."

"Let's go. I'd like to talk over what's been done so far," I say.

He hesitates, and I look at him blankly for a moment before realizing he's not going to say anything.

"Is something wrong?"

"I thought you were going to handle this on your own," he says.

"Like I said, I'm here to wrap up the investigation. I didn't come to wipe it away. You've been working with Callan from the beginning, and now you're working with me. I know you would have preferred to be handed the case yourself, but I'd hope from a professional standpoint you'd be willing to continue putting full effort into the investigation."

"Of course. Thank you."

We go to the small room in the library, and Jackson unlocks it using the key he tells me they found zipped in the pocket of Callan's coat.

"I was able to get some of the notes for the case out of Callan's car. For an FBI agent, she isn't the most forward-thinking when it comes to vehicle security. She has one of those little black magnetic boxes stuck up in the wheel well with a spare key in it," he says.

"Well, even FBI agents can get locked out of their cars," I say.

"True." He gestures at a pile of files and papers on the table. "That's what I was able to find. I don't have access to her house. I think there may be some notes there. This doesn't look like everything."

"She may have had some of them with her when she was injured. It's unlikely she would have brought a lot of notes with her, but it's possible. Especially if she was intending to confront somebody with what she found out. And if that's the case, they probably took it from her. That means we've lost some of the work she did," I say. "We'll have to go over everything and see if we can piece together any of the missing elements unless we can gain access to her house."

I take off my coat and drape it over a chair before settling in and pulling one of the files toward me. My stomach rumbles, and I realize I haven't eaten yet today and it's getting on into the afternoon. Not wanting to leave the library and waste time I should be spending familiarizing myself with the case so I can determine how to move forward, I order lunch for delivery and jump into the files.

It isn't long before I come across the name Laurie Harrison.

"What do you know about the relationship Danielle Scherer had with her professor?" I ask.

"I don't really know much about it. Callan talked to him. I don't think she believed he had anything to do with it."

I look through her notes about the professor, and my mind goes back to the case that darkened my Christmas season. A professor and student were at the center of that case as well. It's hard not to compare the two cases and consider just how differently such a seemingly similar situation can turn out.

The notes Callan left aren't particularly easy to decipher. She didn't write them out in full sentences or with much cohesion anyone else could understand. Instead, they're more a conglomeration of thoughts, words, and occasional scribbles collected under various headings to keep them organized. I'm going to need to speak with everyone she spoke to and compare it to what she has jotted down to try to piece everything together and give it meaning.

I am both far ahead in this investigation and at the very beginning because I have all this information she has gathered, but I can't ask her for clarification or what any of it means. She's still unconscious in the hospital, and until she's able to speak to me, all I have to go on is what I can take from her notes and what Jackson can tell me.

"I don't know if you've looked much at Callan's notes, but they are definitely not easy to interpret. I'm really going to rely on you to help me figure some of it out," I tell him.

Jackson looks hesitant. "I'm willing to help you in any way I can, but I don't know how much help that would be. I haven't been as… involved in the case as Callan was."

"What do you mean you haven't been as involved in the case?" I ask. "I know you weren't there when she was at the river, but what else haven't you done?"

"Callan was the lead, and I had other things on my mind," he says. "She did most of the investigation on her own. I was involved in some of it, but there are things in her notes that I don't know about."

"So when I asked you why she was down at the river by herself and you said you didn't know, the better answer would probably have been that you hadn't been acting as her partner during this case and that resulted in her making that decision," I say.

"It isn't my fault she went down there by herself and ended up hurt," Jackson says. "You can't blame me for her bad decisions."

"I'm not blaming you for her decisions. Those were hers to make. I'm pointing out basic facts. You decided to separate yourself from this case from the beginning because Eric Martinez decided to put Callan in the lead for this case rather than you. It made you angry that she was put ahead of you."

Jackson squirms a bit, but finally relents. "Yes. As predictable as it is, yes, it did sting that he decided to put her in the lead if I was going to be her partner. I've been in a Bureau far longer than she has, and I've proven myself. But that doesn't mean I don't acknowledge her skills and recognize that sometimes the seniority doesn't fall into place. I didn't resent her. But I've worked with her before, and I've heard from others who have worked with her. She likes to do things her way, and she is stubborn as hell. She'll play nice when she has to for the most part, but she wants to do things how she sees them. I figured if she was going to be in charge, she could get what she wanted."

"You know that's petty as hell, right?" I ask. "You compromised an investigation, which ended up putting your partner's life at risk, her weapon going missing, and a serial killer getting away again, because you wanted to prove a point."

"It isn't that simple," he says. "But yes, I know I should have been more involved, and I know I should have been with her that night, and I feel like shit about it. That's one of the main reasons I got as upset as I did that Agent Martinez didn't let me take charge of the case. I already feel like a failure. I already feel like I completely fucked up, and I don't even have the opportunity to make it better."

"You can't fix it. I'm not even going to stand here and pretend that you can. What you can do is commit yourself to this case and help me stop the person who did this. It won't repair the damage that's been done. But it can stop more from happening," I say.

My phone rings, and I see it's Detective Tarrant.

"What can I do for you, Detective?" I ask.

"Asher Vance has been found," she says.

My muscles tighten in preparation for further news. "Is he alive?"

"Yes. He's injured and has been admitted to the hospital, but he is alive."

"Thank you."

CHAPTER TWENTY-THREE

Asher Vance is attached to an IV, and he has a couple of bandages as well as some bruising on his face. His condition isn't nearly as severe as Callan's, and he's conscious, though the doctor has told me he was dazed when he first got there and seemed to be struggling with some memory loss.

"I don't have much to tell you. I wish I did," he tells me after I introduce myself and explain why I'm here. "I don't remember what happened. I have some vague, hazy flashes of being attacked, but I couldn't tell you who it was or even exactly what they did."

"Fortunately, you seem to have gotten through it fairly well. I'm glad to see your injuries aren't more serious," I say.

"I am devastated to hear about Agent Thorne. If I had known something was going to happen to her…"

His voice trails off, and I give him a quizzical look. "What? If you had known something was going to happen to her, what?"

"I only mean I feel like something could have gone differently if I had spoken up. You see, in the days leading up to my attack, I was experiencing some harassment and believed I was being stalked. I didn't bring it up to anyone because I didn't want to muddy the case. That type of behavior didn't align with the experience of the other victims. As far as I could tell, none of the other victims have been threatened or stalked leading up to their deaths, so I didn't make the link," he says.

"Three people have been murdered, and you didn't I think it would be important to let investigators know you were being stalked?" I ask.

"You have to understand, Agent Griffin, this wasn't the first time something like this happened to me. I've experienced this kind of thing a few times before. It's an unfortunate side effect of the work I've done," he says.

"As a ... psychology teacher?" I ask, unsure if I'm following him correctly. The comment is odd, and I wonder where he's going with it.

"With all due respect, I'm far more than your average, run-of-the-mill psychology teacher. I don't think anybody has come after me because of my position at the school. But I am a well-educated, well-read, influential consultant. I have been instrumental in several major cases. My insights and the research I've done have been used in a variety of situations, including murder cases. I am not as subtle and discreet as I perhaps should be in some situations. It means people have put a target on me," he says.

"Obviously, I understand that, Mr. Vance," I say. "I'm just not sure how it applies, considering this situation specifically. You just said you didn't tell the police or even Callan that you thought you were being threatened because you didn't think it had anything to do with the investigation. But now you're saying you think it did? Because Callan was injured, you believe your attack was also orchestrated by the same person?" I ask.

"Asher, please," he says. "Yes, that's exactly what I think. If I hadn't been so reluctant to believe the threats against me were being done by the same person, I could have told Agent Thorne, and maybe something could have been done. Now that I've been attacked, I believe the killer found out about my investigation and didn't like how close I was getting to finding proof. He wanted to eliminate me so that I couldn't find that proof and bring it to the attention of the investigators."

"Three people are dead, and Callan Thorne was very nearly the fourth. Your injuries are relatively minor compared to those."

"Like I said, I don't remember everything that happened, and I can't pretend I know everything my attacker was thinking. I can only guess he was trying to garner attention with my disappearance to act as a distraction. Fortunately, my in-depth understanding of abductions, assaults, and murders gave me a very niche set of knowledge and skills that enabled me to survive and escape," he says. "I only wish I could remember everything so I could know if I was on the right track."

"What track is that?" I ask.

"I believe I've gotten very close to proving the identity of the killer. Agent Thorne had her own suspicions as well. Connections to the victims. Opportunity. Strange behavior. All hallmarks of a killer in the throes of a binge, so to speak. It hurts me even more to think that if I warned her… I don't want to say anything that might influence you, Agent Griffin. I know it's important for you to execute your own investigation. But if you're interested, you are welcome to my notes. Maybe they would be helpful to you," he says. He pauses and seems to think for a few seconds. "Was Agent Blanchard able to give any details about Agent Thorne's attack? Maybe who she was going to see?"

There is a slight inflection in the way he says this that suggests Jackson isn't involved in the case anymore and that this is significant.

"No, I say. When I spoke to him, he said he did not know why she was where she was and what might have happened. He's currently going through her notes to help me better understand her approach to the investigation."

"He's still involved in the investigation?" Asher asks.

"He is," I say.

"Go to my office at the university. There's a key under the desk calendar. That's the key to the top drawer. You'll find my notes there. If you have any questions about them, please don't hesitate to call me. I'm hoping to be out of here soon, and I would be happy to go over any of my notes or help you in any way that I can," he says.

"Thank you," I say. "I really appreciate your cooperation. I'm glad to see you were able to defend yourself and get away."

"I just hope it's enough," he says.

The comment lingers with me as I make my way to the university. The building hallways are familiar, and I find Asher Vance's office easily. The door is locked, but Asher has given me the key so I'm able to let myself in. I'm surprised he keeps his key under the large calendar in the middle of the desk. It seems like such a simplistic place to hide it, like the first place someone would look if they were trying to find the key to unlock the drawer. At the same time, that would require them to know what they were looking for and where to find it, which would be unlikely.

THE GIRL AND THE SECRET PASSAGE

I open the drawer and take out a thick stack of notebooks and files. It looks like Asher was diving into this case even more deeply than what he was presenting to the class. He'd become intent on understanding every step of it and trying to narrow down the options of who it might have been.

As I'm leaving the office, I notice a book on one of the shelves sticking slightly out of place so it hangs over the edge. It doesn't look like it belongs with the others, and I take it out of its place.

Flipping through the pages, I find a passage underlined in blood.

CHAPTER TWENTY-FOUR

"We need to go back to the spot where Agent Thorne was found and move out in a radius from there. She was likely not attacked in that exact spot but entered the water in another location and was moved by the current. Search carefully."

The team of officers Detective Tarrant assembled nods, and I look at her.

"Please keep in touch. Agent Blanchard is your point of contact if I'm not available."

"I will."

I hurry out of the police station and back to my car. My discovery of the bloodied book has triggered a search for another body. It seems logical that the body would be located somewhere near Callan's attack, but I'm honestly not completely sure. She could have gone to confront the killer at that location for a different reason. Right now what matters is finding the victim. I want to be a part of the search, but I need to push further in the investigation. As I head for the university library, I call the hospital to speak with Asher Vance.

"*King Arthur?*" he asks when I tell him about the book. I avoid telling him the specifics of the quote, but I need to know about that particular book. "You found that in my office? No. That wouldn't usually be on my shelf. It's not one that I've been reading, personally. And I didn't take it out of the library. Was it in order with the rest of the books? I have a fairly obvious organizational approach."

"I honestly didn't take the time to try to interpret your organizational approach, but the reason it caught my attention is it did look out of place. It was sticking out slightly from the shelf, and the rest of the books were not," I tell him.

"Then somebody must have put it there. My assistant, Marcus, has full access to the office. But it's also often left unlocked during office hours even if we aren't there so students can leave work and notes for us. Anybody who knew that, or anybody who simply asked about it, could have put the book there," he says.

I thank him and end the call abruptly. I don't have the space and my thoughts right now to continue the conversation. I'm trying to piece together who could have put a book in the professor's office without somebody noticing. There are no cameras in the hallways, so there's no way to see who might have gone in. Depending on the time of day, there also could have been nobody else around, which would mean there would be no witnesses. I think back on what I heard about Asher's disappearance, including Callan going to the office and finding the assistant.

At this point, Marcus is looking very suspicious.

When I'm back at the library, I get a call from Jackson telling me the team of officers is organized, their plan for the search is finalized, and they are leaving for the location. He is going to be there to participate in the search but will also be in charge, acting as a touch point in case there are questions or if anything is found.

"I talked to Vance," I tell him. "He says he doesn't recognize that book. That he would have no reason to have it. That somebody else must have put it into the office."

"His assistant, Marcus?" Jackson asks.

"He did mention that he has full access to the office," I say. "But that seems so obvious. It's one of those quandaries that you hit in an investigation where something that seems far too predictable, far too obvious, to actually be the explanation, but then that makes you think that could then be the explanation because it would seem so obvious that it couldn't be it. Marcus could have known that hiding the book in Asher's office would immediately point to him, which would mean that the suspicion wouldn't fall on him because why would somebody as intelligent as him do something so obvious? Which would, of course, mean that would be what he was doing."

As the words come out of my mouth, I realize how much I sound like Xavier. It would be the exact type of observation he would have come up with, and it makes full sense. Often it's difficult to tell the difference between somebody doing something brilliant and absolutely asinine. That's the line we have to draw in an investigation.

"I'll call you if I can think of anything," Jackson says, and we end the call.

I had intended to work my investigation starting with where most investigations start: talking to people about the victims and the chain of events leading up to their deaths. It's obvious to me now, though, that these clues from the books are the center of the case. I have to focus on them and be able to understand what they mean for them to become a trail that will lead to the killer.

I have the cards Callan made of the passages, and I make a new one to include the most recent. I notice a piece of paper with a handwritten quote on it, but it doesn't have any context. It isn't in Callan's handwriting. I set it aside and go to work laying out the rest of the cards to put together a timeline. I need to understand how these passages flow from one to the next. I have the notes and the research Callan left, as well as the notes from Asher Vance and his class to give me as much context as possible. I know Callan was keeping the passages themselves confidential, so the commentary from the professor and students is based purely on the victims and the titles of the books that had been leaked by others that he knew about.

Reading through Asher's notes is an eye-opening experience that gives even more credence to his theory that someone was so offended by his work they would attack him even outside of the context of the serial killings. Callan's notes might have been difficult to decipher because of the way she wrote them down, but his are difficult to read because of their content. The commentary and theories filling the notebooks and papers he let me take out are nothing short of scathing and judgmental. While a lot of people tend to hold back and show a tremendous amount of restraint and even reality-revising respect when it comes to murder victims, Asher Vance seems to feel no such compulsion.

He is brutally honest and straightforward in his thoughts about each of the victims and what might have contributed to their murders. But it isn't just streams of condemnation and criticism. Everything he says uses references to existing cases and precedents to justify the commentary on each of the victims—including their perceived deceit, promiscuity, lack of accountability, and entitlement.

Trying to keep those ideas in mind and use them as a framework for understanding the killer's choice of victims, I read back through Callan's explanations and evaluations of the passages. The progression of the clues from torn paper to bloodied passage to another torn paper again makes sense, but while some of the passages line up with that, the others feel awkward or forced. There are several leaps in logic she made that I can't wrap my head around.

I keep going over the passages again and again, looking at the victims and the lives they were living at the time of their deaths to try to find the right thread, the key that is going to make it click into place. Finally, I realize this isn't doing any good. I'm too worked up and thinking too much about the search for the body. I decide to take a break from the clues and the research and join the search. I can offer a different perspective in the search, and maybe it will give my brain a chance to work on and start sifting through the massive deluge of information I just poured into it.

The area near the river is very different now from when I stood there in the murky gray this morning. It's getting dark, and while streetlights strive to offer some respite in the blackness, far more illumination is coming from the officers' flashlights as they search. It was so empty here when I stood at the edge of the water and looked down at the lonely place where she'd been found. Now it's crawling with people and tense with energy and activity.

There are obviously plenty of people searching here, so I get back in my car and move further down toward the canal walk. The search is starting to attract attention from people who are lining up along the edge of the road to watch. Some of them are shouting questions at us, and I can't help but wonder if people who do that expect to actually get answers. I don't get much time to think about it.

I've been at the search for less than an hour and am getting an update from Jackson when a shout from the edge of the water makes us break into a run. We get to the water in time to see three officers pulling something out of the water. A moment later the body of a man, his legs tied together and weighted down, is laid out on the grass.

CHAPTER TWENTY-FIVE

Standing in the morgue looking down at the body of Raul Mercer, I can't help but feel something is off. A thirty-year-old tour guide for one of the boat rides down the canal, Mercer doesn't seem to fit in with anyone else. It almost feels like he isn't a victim of the same killer, that discovering his body has been a coincidence. But anybody who knows my husband will know the exact sentence that is repeating through my mind as soon as that comes into my thoughts.

There's no such thing as coincidences.

Sam is steadfast in his belief about this, but sometimes it's hard to really reconcile the idea that everything is falling into some sort of exact pattern for a reason and the reality of what is happening. If this man weren't killed by the same person as the other three, finding his body would have no context. Most people would call that a coincidence. Sam would say it was supposed to happen that way. Even if that's true, that doesn't help my investigation. It doesn't make it make any more sense.

"Can you make any guesses on the cause of death yet?" I ask the medical examiner.

"Right now it looks like a fairly straightforward case of blunt-force trauma to the head. There aren't any defensive wounds or anything that suggests mutual combat prior to the blow. The angle also indicates it was delivered from behind. Likely this man didn't even see his killer," she says.

"What about this?" I ask, indicating a small but deep cut on the inside of Raul's arm. "Is that from something in the water? A rock?"

"Unlikely. The area where he was found doesn't have the kind of sharp rocks and debris that the rest of the river does. And even if he did get caught on something or something hit him while he was under the water, the wound would be more of a tearing or ripping type, most likely. The edges would be rougher. This wound is clean and quite deep. Almost like a stab. It's very intentional."

"So probably done with a knife or something similar," I say.

"Probably," she agrees. "It shows indications that it was done after death. So it wasn't a tactic to get him under control or anything."

That doesn't surprise me. What I see when I look at that wound is a source of blood to be collected.

"Please let me know when your full examination is done. I'd also appreciate any information you can give me on the other victims," I say.

Armed with the information from the medical examiner, I go back to the library. I'm exhausted after barely sleeping between the discovery of the body last night and meeting with the medical examiner this morning, but I can't force myself to stop and rest. This situation is escalating quickly, and I need to get it under control.

Jackson is waiting at the library with coffee when I arrive.

"Anything new?" I ask.

While I was talking to the medical examiner, he was back at the police station talking to the crime scene investigation unit and Detective Tarrant.

"Nothing significant. Mercer went to work the night Callan was attacked, and nobody had heard from him after he finished his last tour. He wasn't married and didn't have any children, so it wasn't until his brother tried to get in touch with him yesterday that anyone even realized something was wrong. He had actually called the station to report his brother missing just a couple of hours before his body was found. Right now it looks like maybe Callan figured out who the next victim was and what was going to happen, went to confront the killer, but was too late. Raul had already been killed, then he attacked Callan, tossed her into the water thinking she was dead, and left," he tells me.

Jackson sounds completely confident in this theory of events, but it doesn't sit well with me. Something about it just doesn't feel right.

"His body was tied to weights. That isn't something that just happens at the spur of the moment. And it doesn't happen when there are people around. In order for that theory to work out, the killer would have had to have been in the process of killing Raul when Callan got there. He set that aside to engage Callan in a pretty brutal attack and tossed her into the water somewhere that would bring her down the river a bit to get stuck on those rocks. He then went back to Raul, tied him to the weights, and put him in the water without anyone noticing," I say.

I run my fingers back through my hair and let out a breath. "These passages. They're just not making sense the way they're supposed to. The killer obviously chose them intentionally. There are too many links between the words themselves for them to just be random quotes he found somewhere. And there's a progression. It does go from quote to quote, and Callan was able to make some connections. Unfortunately, we don't always get to know what's in the mind of a serial killer. While it might seem like there is an obvious step-by-step trail that's supposed to be followed, that might not be why he chose them this way.

"Some killers merely want to leave things like this behind for their own purposes. They aren't offering clues. They aren't even always taunting investigators. Sometimes it's just a matter of ritual. They are making the experience more satisfying for themselves."

My phone chirps beside, me and I see a text.

Xavier: *Is there a vending machine in the library?*

I smile a little at the message. It's a reminder of the first time I met him, the encounter that showed me this man was nothing like anyone I'd ever known and yet wasn't the delusional, unbalanced monster he was being made out to be. I'm not sure why he sent the message. Maybe just his way of telling me he's thinking about me.

Emma: *I think so.*

Xavier: *Where?*

Now I feel a little like he's leading me into a thought exercise I haven't agreed to. That would not be a new experience.

Emma: *I think it's in the basement near the technology lab.*

Xavier: *That's a good place to have a snack.*

Emma: *Am I supposed to go to the vending machine?*

Xavier: *I don't know, Emma, are you?*

I read the message a couple of times, playing the fun game all of us get roped into of trying to sort out what Xavier actually means as opposed to what the words seem to suggest he means.

"Is everything okay?" Jackson asks.

"Um, yeah. I'll be right back."

"Should I come with you?" he asks.

"No, I'm not leaving the building."

I take my phone and leave the study room. The steps leading down into the basement are in the back corner of the library, and I catch the door just as it swings closed behind a group of students who have come out of it. I've gone down several steps when I hear the door at the bottom close. A flash in my memory of the masked figure in the police station makes me pause. The footsteps coming up toward me don't sound hurried or particularly slow. It's just someone climbing the steps.

A few steps later, I see a familiar head coming toward me. He's looking down into a bag in his hands and not paying any attention to where he is going, which is exactly what I would expect.

"Xavier?"

Xavier's face snaps up, and a little smile curves his lips. "Hey, Emma."

"You're here?" I ask.

He looks at the bag of chips in his hand and then glances behind him like he's looking back toward the basement.

"Why did you think I asked you where the vending machine was?" he asks. "I guess you decided you're hungry. I'll walk with you back there. There's a pretty good selection. No peanuts. I guess for inclusiveness."

He turns around unceremoniously and starts back to the basement. I watch him for a couple of steps, then follow, jumping down a couple at a time to catch up with him. It isn't lost on me that he could not be here by himself. But he does appear to be roaming the library alone.

"Who else is here? Is Dean here?" I ask as I'm going through the door he's holding open for me.

"He and Sam decided to take the elevator up. I don't do unfamiliar elevators," he says.

"I'm aware," I say. "Sam? Sam is here?"

He stares at me and blinks. "Yes. Let's get you a snack."

By the time we get to the vending machine, Dean is already calling Xavier trying to find out where he has ended up and Sam is calling me trying to find out where I am.

"They are together," Dean says to Sam, causing his voice to come out of both phones.

Xavier promptly hits the button to end the call and stuffs his phone in his pocket. Hearing the same voice come from multiple sources is apparently a hard no for Xavier.

I collect a few snacks and drinks, and we go back up the steps, meeting Dean and Sam just outside the door.

"What are you guys doing here? I ask, accepting a kiss from my husband and a hug from my cousin.

"We all decided we needed a break and thought to ourselves, 'What is more traditional for early January than a visit to Richmond?'" Sam says.

"There is literally nothing traditional about an early January visit to Richmond," I say.

"Which is what we told him," Dean says.

"I thought it was a very creative way to manipulate us into coming to visit you," Xavier says as though he thinks it's very sweet.

"I'm really glad you're here. Not just because I missed you, but I could use some fresh perspective There's been another murder. But it doesn't make any sense. It doesn't fit in with the other ones. Which is making me wonder whether it's actually that murder that doesn't fit or if it's the established understanding of all of them that isn't correct."

"Or both," Xavier says.

"Exactly," I say. "Come on. I'll bring you to the war room and introduce you to Callan's partner."

I do the round of introductions and make a pile of the snacks and drinks off the side of the table so everyone has easy access to them. I show the guys the timeline I've been making with the passages and go over it.

"This is... pretty confusing," Dean says.

"It is," I say. "But I don't think it's supposed to be. At least not in a nonsensical way. I think it's meant to make us think. I honestly believe there is a progression here, there is a step-by-step trail we're supposed to be following. Or at the very least, that exists to amuse the killer."

"Like some sort of morbid letterboxing expedition," Xavier says. He sees Jackson staring at him and stares back for several seconds of tense silence. "It's a kind of scavenger hunt. People put clues up on the internet, and other people follow them to find boxes. But generally, those boxes contain delightful stamps, not corpses."

"None of these victims have been in boxes," Jackson says.

Xavier turns slowly and looks at me. According to Xavier, in this circumstance, Jackson is an extension of me, so I am responsible for making sure his communication makes sense. And it's just a little bit my fault that he doesn't understand Xavier because I am choosing to be in proximity of him. Most of the time, I would at least try to smooth it over, but right now I just don't have the time.

"This passage in particular bothers me," I say, jumping over the awkward moment and going right back into the notes. "'Beware; for I am fearless, and therefore powerful.'"

"That's the one that led us to the mural," Jackson says. "And then we found the artist's body."

"Right," I say. "But that doesn't make sense. This is a quote by Mary Shelley, so I understand the jump, but the quote doesn't say anything about a monster. It's just from the book. And it led to a mural that didn't have any monsters on it, just large animals. And while it did lead to a body being found, the body wasn't at the mural. There was a wide search, and the body was found in an area where that person was known to be on a fairly regular basis. It feels like you stumbled on the body, like it was accidental." I look at Sam. "Note I said 'accidental.'"

"Not a monster," Xavier says.

"But we found a body," Jackson says, his voice overlapping Xavier's. "We followed that clue and found a victim. How does that not fit in with the progression?"

"He wasn't a monster," Xavier says.

"Like I said, a body was found. I acknowledged that. A victim was located by going to that mural. But there was nothing actually at the mural to indicate where the body was. And in the case of the other two victims, nothing about the quotes pointed to a place where they would be found or had a multistep search. The passages aren't meant to say where the bodies are, just that there are bodies."

"Does that mean you don't think that Gray Dove was actually a victim?" Jackson asks.

"He wasn't a monster, Emma," Xavier says more insistently.

"I know, Xavier. He was an artist and was probably misunderstood," I say.

"I can't really speak on that, considering I haven't had much time to critically analyze his work, and I don't have a very strong foundation in constructive artistic critique in the medium of aluminum cans and discarded plastic bags. I'm talking about the quote. Frankenstein. He wasn't a monster," Xavier says.

"He was a bunch of different people sewn up together and shocked back to life," Jackson says. "So are you saying he was a patchwork human? And didn't he go on to kill a bunch of people?"

"Dean," Xavier says.

Dean moves around behind Xavier from where he's been standing, positioning himself on the other side of Xavier so he's further distanced from Jackson. That's not a great sign.

"Damn. I can't believe I didn't think about that," I mutter.

"What?" Jackson asks.

"That's not Frankenstein," Xavier says tightly. "That's Frankenstein's monster. Frankenstein's monster was a monster. Frankenstein was a doctor. He was the one who was fearless and powerful."

"Gray Dove wasn't powerful. And he definitely wasn't a doctor," I say. I shake my head as I look over the passages again. "It isn't just the interpretation of that passage. It's the clues. They're in the wrong order. Look, there are too many leading up to Gray Dove, and there are loose ends that haven't been connected. They didn't just stumble on the death of the artist. He was a victim. He was just in the wrong order."

"What do you mean?" Jackson asks.

"He wasn't supposed to be found yet. Look at this one. This quote is about people obsessing over consumer items and not recognizing true worth in anything. That fits the artist. He took things people threw away and made them into something beautiful. He was nonviolent by nature and tried to make the world better for everyone in it. He wasn't a monster. He didn't think of himself as powerful. We're missing a body."

"We need to be looking for a doctor," Jackson says, realization sinking in. "One that's been dead for several days."

We immediately go to work asking Detective Tarrant to look through missing persons reports and searching for any indication of doctors or other medical personnel in the area who are missing. Within a few hours, we've determined no one fitting the description has been reported missing. We start a larger canvas, checking in with every doctor in the area. It's a painstaking process, but it results in learning there are a few who are on vacation or on work trips who would need to be tracked down, but other than that, everyone is accounted for.

By the time I'm priming myself with coffee the next morning, we have a name. Dr. Dwayne Brown. He was supposed to travel to a conference last week the day before the Mary Shelley clue was found but has not been seen there. He hasn't checked into his hotel room, and his ID badge hasn't been picked up at registration.

"Find his house," I say. "Check the garage."

CHAPTER TWENTY-SIX

We find Dr. Brown's body found in his car, still parked in his garage. The key is in the ignition, and there is luggage in the back seat. A travel coffee tumbler, spotted with mold, is in the cup holder beside him. It looks like he got ready for his trip, got in the car, and was killed before opening the door. The cause of death was a single bullet wound to the side of his head. Decomposition along with the signs of him preparing for his trip prove he's been dead for several days.

"It's out of order," I say after coming back from talking to the detective and the medical examiner about Dr. Brown's death. "Callan's investigation got the order of the bodies wrong. But the order of the passages is also wrong, because there are too many in between the victims. We have to find the right order to make the connections."

The study room Callan was using and that I've inherited from her is too small to lay out the evidence the way I need to, so I move into a conference room with more table space. This allows me to take all the cards with the passages along with pages of notes associated with each victim and lay them out to provide a visual. I walk up and down the table, trying to make connections. Jackson arrives shortly after, having gone to talk to the medical staff who worked with the doctor.

"I was able to get some information about him from the staff, but they wouldn't talk about any patients. However, I spoke with a good friend of his and a colleague. While they wouldn't confirm it by name, they heavily implied Danielle Scherer was under Dr. Brown's care a couple of times," he says.

"A couple of times?" I asked. "He wasn't her usual doctor?"

"No, that's what made it so notable. When she was murdered, they took note because they knew she had seen this doctor a couple of times. Again, they wouldn't come right out and say it, but it was very clear what they were talking about. We're going to have to get a court order for her medical records to approve it, but I can almost guarantee you that's what the connection is. She went to him for care on just a couple of occasions a few months ago," Jackson says.

"Why?" I asked. "Why would she need to go to a different doctor? She lives here in the city. She should have her own physician, and if she doesn't, there's a student health center where she can see the doctor."

"Maybe it was for something she didn't want her regular doctor to know about," Dean suggests.

I gather up a few things and put them in my bag. "Keep going over this here. I'm going to go talk to Nathan Garrett. According to Callan's notes, he was the closest person to her. Maybe he'll know what's going on."

The second I mention the doctor to Nathan, it's obvious he knows something but doesn't want to talk about it.

"I'm sorry," I say. "I know this isn't easy for you to talk about. And it's hard to deal with a new agent after you made a connection with Callan, but I really need your help. If you know anything about this doctor and why Danielle went to see him, I need to know. It could have something to do with her murder."

"I don't know for sure," he says. "She didn't want to talk to me about it, which is part of why I knew it was so serious. We talked about everything. We always had. Since we met, we didn't have secrets between us. Like I told Callan, Danielle and I were best friends from the very beginning, and I loved her deeply. When she became really withdrawn and didn't want to tell me what was going on, I knew something was bad. I didn't want to push her and force her to talk about anything she didn't want to, but there were enough clues that I could figure it out. I think

Professor Harrison got her pregnant. And I think she went to Dr. Brown to get an abortion."

My stomach twisted into a hard, burning knot. The perfect, pristine image of Danielle as a happy woman living a dreamy life is chipping away. It was like looking at an antique porcelain doll. From a distance, there's beauty and perfection. But if you get closer, you can see all the cracks. I ache for her and the pain she must've been going through without anybody around her knowing.

I thank Nathan and leave him sitting on his couch, his arms folded tightly over his stomach as he leans over, staring down at the floor like he's lost in his grief. I wish I could have comforted him, but we've already lost so much time. The killer is even further ahead than we've thought, and piercing together just what happened and how has just gotten harder.

I find Laurie Harrison in his office.

"Professor Harrison?" I say as I enter the room.

"I'm Laurence Harrison," he says in confirmation.

"I'm Agent Emma Griffin. I have taken over the investigation for Callan Thorne," I introduce myself.

"Yes," he says. "It's horrible what happened to her. Is she all right?"

"She's better," I say. "I'm going to cut right to the chase here because I really don't have time to be delicate. I'm here because I went through her notes, and I know what the two of you talked about. I know you were in a relationship with Danielle Scherer. And I need to talk to you about something very sensitive but potentially extremely important."

He takes a deep breath. "All right."

"I don't know if you've heard the news that a fourth victim has been found," I say.

His eyes widen, and he shakes his head. "No, I haven't heard that."

"Dr. Dwayne Brown. He was actually killed right after Danielle. Does that name sound familiar to you?" I ask.

He hesitates. I can see how torn he is.

"I know this isn't something you want anyone to know about. It's probably something you wanted to put far behind you and never have to think about again. But that's not really an option anymore."

"Yes," he finally says. "That's a doctor I brought Danielle to."

"Because she was pregnant," I say.

"Yes," he confirms.

"And she went to Dr. Brown for an abortion?"

Professor Harrison's eyes grow dark, and his eyebrows pull together. He shakes his head.

"No, she didn't have an abortion. Danielle wanted to have the baby. We were just trying to figure out what we were going to do and how we were going to make it all work out. She didn't intend to hide it from anybody. She hadn't talked to Nathan much about it because it would obviously cause difficulties and hurt him. They had been together for a long time, and this would clearly cause the end of their relationship.

"It wasn't an easy situation. She was happy thinking about us being a family in the future, but she was struggling with what it meant for our lives as we knew them. It was obviously going to cause some serious impact. And she didn't want people to find out yet, especially her parents. They were unloving and unsupportive, and she didn't want to deal with the stress of telling them. And even though they treated her poorly, they were still her family. She'd been trying for years to find a way to connect with them, unsuccessfully for the most part, and she knew this would be the final straw for them."

That revelation makes me understand Danielle better. Growing up with parents like that would be a strong motivation for her to fall into a relationship with an older authority figure. Though listening to the way Professor Harrison talks about her and reading the notes Callan left does make it seem that in this instance, he really did love her and thought they would have a future together. It's a stark contrast from my last case involving a professor and student. They are both heartbreaking, but in such different ways.

"She didn't want people to know yet, so that's why you went to Dr. Brown rather than the student health clinic?" I ask.

"Yes. She didn't want to go to the clinic and have them find out about her pregnancy. But also, I wouldn't be able to get involved if she did go there. I couldn't exactly walk into a university-provided clinic and be a happy father-to-be alongside the former student I was in a relationship with. There were rumors about us, but that wasn't exactly the way I wanted to address them. So I paid for her to go to a private doctor to receive prenatal care. But she ended up having a very traumatic miscarriage. It was horrible for both of us, but truly dangerous for her. She was deeply hurt by it, and it impacted a lot of her life. I think she was starting to feel better just before her death, but she was never fully the same person again."

I leave the professor with both answers and questions. This discovery creates another link in the chain of events and connects the victims, but I'm still left wondering how everyone is really connected and what it is that has caused them specifically to be the victims of this vicious killer.

CHAPTER TWENTY-SEVEN

B Y THE END OF THE DAY, I HAVE COVERED THE WALLS OF THE CONference room with butcher paper so I can make my diagrams. For the next two days, I spend every moment delving into the meaning of the passages from the books. I research the books themselves as well as look at the passages from different angles. I think about the actual quotes, the words as what they mean within the context of the book, what they might mean without the context, the history of the writers. Everything I can think of, I find out so I can break these passages down into their smallest pieces and rebuild them in some sort of meaning.

The more I find out, the more I'm able to piece together a six-degrees-of-separation style of progression that connects the victims and the passages from the books. I stand with Jackson in front of one of the diagrams, adding details he's brought from interviews he conducted.

"Warren Mason is kind of dangling. We don't know why he was the first victim and the beginning of all this. But we do know that he knew the second victim, Danielle Scherer, from the coffee shop where she worked. It doesn't seem like they had an ongoing relationship or anything, but they interacted. That leads us to the third victim, which is Dr. Dwayne Brown. Originally, we thought it was the artist, but it's actually the doctor. She knew him because he provided care for her," I say.

"And Dr. Brown knew Gray Dove from his work at the free clinic and because he was a strong proponent of his art," Jackson adds.

"Exactly. So that strings those together. But we haven't been able to find anything that connects Raul Mercer to any of them. We haven't been able to find any instance of any of the victims ever taking one of the canal boat rides, much less one with him as the tour guide. He didn't go to school here. He didn't live near any of them. There is absolutely nothing that we've been able to find that links him to the other victims. And that makes me feel even more like he isn't actually connected to them," I say.

"You don't think he was killed by the same killer?"

"No. I do. But I don't think he was the intended victim. I think there was absolutely supposed to be a murder that night, but it was not that tour guide. I went back on the calendar, and I found out that there was a political event at the canal walk that night. A small rally. I found that handwritten quote among the stacks of Callan's papers. I didn't make the connection at first, but I realized there is a note that says 'meeting… papers… quote… Marcus.'

"I talked to him about it, and he said he didn't know what the 'quote' meant, but he thinks the rest was probably referencing the community meeting they were both at to discuss whether the school should close while the investigation is ongoing. She dropped her bag when there was a disruption in the crowd, and some papers spilled out. He helped her clean them up," I say. "But later on, she found a quote in her bag."

"Why would she make a note about that unless she thought he put it there?" Jackson asks.

"Which brings me to the quote. *Nineteen Eighty-Four.* Are you familiar with it?" I ask.

"I've heard of it," Jackson says. "I think I read it in high school, but honestly, that time of my life is a bit of a blur, and I didn't hang on to a lot of what I learned in classes like English."

"Fair enough. I'll give you a brief breakdown. Essentially, it is a futuristic dystopian novel discussing the breakdown of society based on totalitarian control of the government."

"So… politics," Jackson says. "Like the rally."

"Yes, but that also has to do with the quotes about tomorrow. The politicians who are trying to get elected now are trying to influence tomorrow. However, the specific quote that was written on that piece of paper is about controlling the past and the present. It's about being in control of historical narrative. If you control the present, if you can manipulate and make people do as you say and think what you tell them to in the present, you can then control their view of the past. You can change the past according to their thoughts.

"I think that's a specific reference to the killer. I think Callan figured out the next kill was intended to be the politician speaking at the rally. Something about his policies was offensive to the killer, and he intended to end the possibility that that person could be 'tomorrow.' In that way, the killer was seeking to control the future. But his kills are intended to change the past, also affecting the future."

"Holy shit," Jackson mutters as he looks over the diagram, then a troubled expression crosses his face. "The torn book found in Callan's apartment was the warning for that kill. But the blood-underlined book in Vance's office means there's going to be another victim."

"I know. Which means we need to end it before that happens."

"Does he think it was me?" Jackson suddenly asks.

I look at him, and he lets out a breath.

"I know he said he was very close to identifying the killer and having proof when he was attacked. There are notes from some of his students who have theories as well. Callan..." He takes another breath. "Callan confronted me and all but accused me of being the killer because I have a connection to the first three victims. At least with the first three she knew about. She didn't know about the doctor."

"Did you know him?"

"I didn't know him. Not personally anyway. I did go to the free clinic once for my flu shot. I guess he could have given me the shot, but I don't know. I didn't have any reason to have anything against him. But I need to know if that's what Vance thinks too," he says.

"He didn't say that," I say. "And it isn't written in his notes. But he did specifically ask if you were still involved in the case. I think he might have been considering you."

Jackson rakes his fingers back through his hair, gripping it at the back of his head for a second as he stares at the wall.

"I didn't do this, Emma."

"I need to talk to him again. I need to ask him straight out if he thinks you are involved and why," I say. "Maybe there's something he noticed that we're not thinking about."

Asher Vance doesn't answer his phone when I call, so I contact the hospital so I can set up a time to talk to him again.

"He's not here anymore," the nurse tells me. "He discharged himself this morning."

"He discharged himself?" I ask incredulously. "He just decided he was leaving?"

"Essentially. The doctor advised him to stay for more observation, but he refused. He said there were important things that he needed to do, that people were depending on him and he needed to get back to campus."

I'm stunned to hear that, and I don't even know if I said goodbye when I hung up the phone. I look at Jackson, who seems shaky and on edge.

"He went back to the school."

CHAPTER TWENTY-EIGHT

Asher Vance is in his office furiously typing on his computer when I walk in. He doesn't even look up.
"I'm sorry. I am busy right now. I appreciate you coming to check on me, but I can't stop, he says.
"I'm not here to check on you," I say.
He looks up, his expression both surprised and delighted.
"Agent Griffin," he says, "I didn't expect to see you here."
"I think I'm the one who should be saying that to you. You should still be in the hospital right now. But I hear you decided to check yourself out so you could come back to campus," I say.
"I didn't really have a choice. The doctor was talking about keeping me for observation and potential further treatments. Who knows how long they could have kept me there? I couldn't waste that time. I couldn't just sit around in the hospital when so much needed to be done. I've already missed two classes. I need to take the information from all of the new developments in the case and prepare for my next

class tonight. Not to mention drawing up the plans for next semester and beyond. This case is so big, and people are looking to me for my insights and expertise to bring it to a close. I couldn't in good conscience sit in that hospital healing from my injuries while other people are in danger," he says.

"That's not something you need to be concerning yourself with," I say. "This case under the purview of the FBI. Your job is to teach psychology. *I* am investigating these murders."

"Using my notes and research," he points out arrogantly.

"I'm using the notes and research from the FBI agent who was initially assigned to this case and was doing an exceptional job with the investigation until she was savagely attacked. I've looked over your notes, but you are not an investigator. As far as I can tell, you pushing yourself into this situation and forcing your involvement has only resulted in you getting attacked."

"I have made huge strides in this case," he says angrily, his face becoming dark and aggressive as all pleasantness drained out of it. "There are elements of it no one would even have thought of if it wasn't for my expertise, my vision. Nurses at the hospital were asking me about it. The police officers were asking me about it."

"That's their job," I point out. "You were found after some unknown assailant did something to you that you can't remember. That's the time for people to ask questions. And when there is a serial killer active in the area, that's going to come up. I assure you, there are plenty of other people who contacted police over the last couple of weeks who were asked about the killings. That doesn't make them involved. And it doesn't make them investigators."

"I might not have a shield, Agent Griffin, but this is my case. It went off the rails from the very beginning with that girl at the helm, and I'm the one who got it under control. The only reason I was attacked was because I was getting far too close for the comfort of her partner, and the only reason I survived was because of my own knowledge, which far exceeds that of both of them."

"Her partner?" I seethe. "Are you accusing an FBI agent of committing these murders?"

He holds up his hands like he's showing me he's innocent and has nothing to hide, but his face smears with a smug grin. "You read the notes. If you came to that kind of conclusion, it should tell you something."

"You need to back off. Your obsession with this case and getting attention for it is dangerous, and you are not important to this investigation." I take a step closer to him. "I don't know who you think you are, but I'm going to tell you who you're dealing with. That girl you mentioned is a highly trained special agent who has learned and experienced things you will only ever dream of even after just a few years of service. Her partner was a police officer who served this city before he went to the Academy and has had an exemplary record within the Bureau since."

"And you?" he asks through gritted teeth, taking a step forward to match mine.

"I'm not impressed."

"Professor!"

A shout breaks the aggressive tension filling the office, and Vance steps around me toward the open door. A second later a boy with frantic eyes runs in, looking wired and on edge.

"Anthony, what is it?" he asks. "What's wrong?"

"I did it," Anthony says. "I did it."

Vance's back straightens, and his eyes snap between the student and me.

"What are you talking about?" he asks. "What did you do?"

"Calm down," I tell him. "Take a deep breath."

"I uncovered a connection in the clues. I was going over everything again, and I figured out who the next victim was supposed to be, and I saved her!"

Heat spreads across my face and the back of my neck. This has just gotten extremely serious.

"That's amazing!" Vance gushes.

"I'm Special Agent Griffin," I say, getting closer to the student to try to distance him from the professor. "I've taken over this investigation. I need you to tell me exactly what happened."

"I can handle this," Vance says, trying to push past me. "This is my student."

"I don't care who he is to you. If he believes he has intercepted a murder in a serial murder case, he is now my witness. Anthony, I need you to tell me exactly what the process was that you followed to figure out who you think the next victim was, who it was, and what happened," I say. "You need to come with me to make a statement to the detectives, and the victim should as well."

"This is ridiculous," Vance says. "Doing all that isn't going to do any good. Right now there is a killer out there who just almost claimed a fifth victim. We should be celebrating the accomplishments of this incredible student and using what he found out to prove who we already know is the killer. Tell me, Agent, where's your partner right now?"

"Be extremely careful what you say," I tell him. "No matter how important you think you are, you are not above defamation of character. And if your implications incite any type of violence, I will make sure you are brought in and charged with as many things as I can possibly come up with, including attempted murder of a federal agent."

He scoffs. "It seems you need a lesson in freedom of speech, Agent."

"Freedom of speech gives you the right to speak openly and express yourself freely without others dictating what that can and cannot include. It doesn't give you the right to say anything you want to without consequences. Perhaps it's you who needs to learn the distinction," I tell him.

"Oh, I'm not stating facts. I am merely pointing out what seems extraordinarily obvious. But there is another option. A certain man reeling over an inappropriate relationship gone wrong. Does that sound familiar?"

"If you were so confident in either of those, you would have already gone to the police to have them arrested. Because you haven't, you know you're not as smart as you thought you were. You have guesses. That's it. And if this student did somehow stumble into a pattern and was able to stop one of these kills from happening, he needs to tell me about it," I say.

"You're slowing us down. All this red tape is just getting in the way of finally being able to nail this killer," Anthony says.

"Come on," Vance says to Anthony.

They start to move toward the door, and I step in front of them.

"I'm going to put it to you this way. Either he tells me what he's talking about here and now, or I have both of you arrested for obstruction of justice, and you can talk to me about it at the station."

Anthony and Asher look at each other and sigh as they come to the same conclusion. We sit down, and I listen to Anthony break down his thought process in evaluating the pieces of evidence available to him. Without the exact passages to go on, all he could do was think about the books he did know about as well as the available information about the victims. As he lays it all out, I realize he sounds logical. When he reveals the name of the potential victim and the circumstances of finding her bound and duct-taped in a rarely used room of the university's theater building, I realize he may have actually thwarted another kill.

"Where is Cassandra now?" I ask when he's finished.

"She's at her dorm. She said she wasn't ready to talk about it and wanted to take a shower and a nap, that maybe after she was feeling better, she would be ready to talk to you. She said she hadn't been raped, so I didn't argue with her. I figured it's her choice. I can't force her to do anything, especially after going through a trauma like that," he says.

I roll my eyes, so worked up by the irresponsible way he's handled the situation that I can't keep sitting. I stand up and pace back and forth across the office.

"Sexual assault isn't the only situation when showering is a bad idea," I say. "Any type of physical contact with an assailant, including something like being duct-taped and presumably carried and forced into a room provides a potential source for fiber evidence, hair evidence, even skin cells and possibly saliva. All of that can be collected from a victim if they are properly and appropriately processed immediately after the crime."

"Processed?" Asher asks. "You make her sound like a piece of meat."

"I'm not the one treating her like a piece of meat," I say. "And for someone who touts himself as being such an impressive mind for crime and the father of the next generation of great investigators, you didn't educate your students particularly well on proper preservation and handling of evidence, or the fact that providing information that could lead to the capture of a serial killer far outweighs the importance of being delicate about somebody's feelings. I expect you to go to the police station and give a statement. I'll let Detective Tarrant know you're coming.

"Both of you are to stay away from Cassandra. I don't want to hear that either one of you called her, texted her, went to visit her. Unless you are talking to me or the detective, you're not even to say her name. Do I make myself very clear?"

By the end of the evening, news that the killer almost claimed another victim has spread through the university. An emergency order has gone out, shutting down campus and commanding students to remain in their dorms except for urgent necessary activities. Faculty and a skeleton staff would continue running basic operations, but in-person classes and activities are canceled for the foreseeable future. I know the chances of many of the students actually complying with that order are very low, but at least some will stay out of harm's way.

As Jackson helps me pack everything to move from the library to the house I'm renting for the duration of my time here, Sam calls. The guys were only able to stay for two days before he had to get back to Sherwood to his responsibilities as sheriff, and Dean needed to push forward with his own case. I'm used to being in the field alone, but I still miss my family when we're apart.

But I don't get the boost of hearing Sam's voice that I was expecting. We're barely able to make our goodbyes before my call gets interrupted by one of the doctors on Callan's medical team. My stomach sinks a little as I prepare for what he has to tell me.

"Callan received a delivery of flowers today," he says.

"Flowers?" I ask, not understanding the significance.

"Yes. They came with a card, and I felt like you needed to hear it," he says.

"All right," I say.

"There isn't a signature or anything. It's just a quote from *To Kill a Mockingbird* by Harper Lee. 'I wanted you to see what real courage is, instead of getting the idea that courage is a man with a gun in his hand.'"

CHAPTER TWENTY-NINE

I DON'T NEED ANYTHING OTHER THAN THOSE WORDS TO KNOW THAT the card is a direct threat from the killer. It confirms to me that Callan was developing a strong theory and had gone down to the canal following her instincts that the politician speaking at the rally that night was going to be attacked. It suggests that the killer had intended for her to witness the murder of the politician, but something happened, and it didn't work out that way. Instead, she ended up witnessing the death of the tour guide and was then attacked. The message is taunting her, telling her that her weapon doesn't compete with his skill and intelligence.

This brings me back to Callan's notes and the locations and dates I found jotted on the margins of one of the pages. There was no indication of what they meant or why she put them there. It looked like she was just quickly recording them so she wouldn't forget, like people do with sudden things they remember they need from the grocery store or the date of an upcoming work activity. It doesn't give me much to actually base research on, but I know it means something. She went down to that canal because she knew something was going to happen. These dates and locations could point to something else she had uncovered.

"Hey," I say to Jackson as he comes back into the room with the bag containing yet another takeaway meal. "You know, I decided to stay in this short-term rental house rather than getting a hotel room because I figured it would be more comfortable and have more amenities I could use. Like a kitchen. So far I've made a lot of coffee and grilled cheese sandwiches. I have all the ingredients to make cinnamon rolls and haven't had the time to do it."

"We are sitting twenty feet away from the kitchen," Jackson points out. "I could hear you talking from there if you want to go make those rolls while we go over things."

He grins at me, and I can't help but laugh.

"All right. After we eat."

"Deal."

"Any luck with the bookstores and libraries?" I ask.

Trying to build on my theory that the tour guide was not the intended victim, I have tasked Jackson to head up contacting all the bookstores and libraries in the area to find out if anyone had recently acquired a copy of George Orwell's *Nineteen Eighty-Four*. I believe it's very likely a copy was purchased so it could have the quote found in Callan's bag underlined in the blood of the victim, but the plan suddenly changed.

"A lot of copies of the book have been purchased or checked out, so we're going through the names of those people now. Unfortunately, some of the purchases were made in cash, so we can't trace those. So far, though, there's nothing to go on."

"All right. We'll just keep looking."

I glance down at the dates and locations again, and Jackson seems to notice.

"What's that?"

"It's another page of Callan's notes. I saw these little notations when I was first going over everything, but they didn't really mean anything. They were written really small and kind of up to the corner, so it almost looks like they don't have anything to do with what's written on the page. Like they were things that just kind of popped into her head and she wrote them down so she wouldn't forget but didn't want to confuse them with the rest of her notes. It's just some locations and dates," I tell him.

He turns the paper toward him. "This one," he says, tapping his finger on the paper, is near where Warren and I went to college. It's basically the residential area right next to campus."

"Really?" I ask.

"Yeah." His voice drops as he stares at the notation. He suddenly starts packing his food back up. "I need to go do something. I'll get in touch with you later."

"Where are you going?" I ask.

"I'll get in touch with you later," he repeats. "Save some cinnamon rolls for me."

I finish eating then bring my computer into the kitchen with me so I can research while I make the rolls. Jackson didn't mention the name of the school, but I quickly search the area and find out there is only one college nearby. On a whim, I search for the college along with the location and date written on the paper. One of the search results instantly grabs me. I finish the dough as fast as I can and put it in the refrigerator. Grabbing the paper and my bag, I head out.

***

My first stop is Stephanie Campano's house. I've already spoken to her briefly just to review what she told Callan, but now I show her what I've found on the computer.

"I recognize that article," she says. "It's one of the ones Asher Vance has hanging up on his office wall."

"He taught at this school," I say. "The same one Warren Mason went to."

"The first victim?" she asks.

"Yes. Apparently, he went to school there at the same time Asher Vance was a psychology professor there. And then he came to be a professor here."

"Not a professor," Stephanie says.

"What do you mean?" I ask. "In Callan's notes it says 'Professor Vance,' and I've heard other people refer to him that way."

"I know. It's kind of an impulse people have for anybody who teaches at a college or university, but technically, he's not a professor here. He's an instructor. If you look at faculty lists and anything that mentions him that comes from the university, he's referred to as Mr.

Vance, not Professor Vance. If I remember correctly, he was a professor at that school, but something happened and derailed his career a bit. I wish I could be more helpful, but he and I haven't ever been close. We know each other professionally, but I wouldn't call him a friend. You might want to talk to Laurie Harrison. He knows Asher far better than I do."

I find Laurie Harrison at the student commons getting coffee from a machine that has been moved out into the open to offer teachers a faster option while the service is closed. He seems in a rush, so I hop into step beside him.

"Asher was a professor before coming here," he confirms. "He hadn't earned tenure yet, but was on track, so that's how he had that title. Unfortunately, there was a lot of unpleasantness surrounding him."

"What do you mean by unpleasantness?" I ask.

"Did Agent Thorne have anything in her notes about how the students felt about him or his classes before this semester?"

"Not really. There's one note that says 'not a favorite,' but I thought that she was talking about her own feelings toward him."

"That's possible, but it's well known that Asher Vance is not a particularly well-liked instructor at the school. His students routinely complain about him and try to avoid taking his classes. He has very little support among faculty members. He's known for being overly hard on his students, to the point of seeming to look for ways to fail them rather than encouraging them to succeed. He's extremely arrogant and emotionally abusive. He has interfered with cases and compromised investigations several times.

"He has those articles up on the walls in his office, but what he won't tell you is, there are many others he has published that contained outright lies and had to be retracted. I've heard people say he was sued a couple of times but ended up settling out of court. He was finally fired after a student submitted a formal complaint against him for his treatment and grading practices. He was apparently outraged. I didn't know him at the time, but I have associates who were in the area, and they say he completely lashed out against the school and everyone around," he tells me.

"How did he possibly get hired here after all that?" I ask.

Harrison shrugs. "I don't know what goes into the decisions, but I'm assuming they talked to him and he was able to manipulate them the same way he manipulates other people. He pushed his accomplishments and brilliance, claiming he was simply misunderstood. They likely gave him a second chance because he can be a very good teacher.

"Unfortunately, he has much of the same reputation here that he did there. He has his followers, but very few students want anything to do with him. Very few faculty members associate with him. He has stopped publishing anything of merit. Some of his older work has been discredited and removed from circulation. He finally seems to have gotten himself together and is doing well teaching with this case, but it's too little too late. He isn't a professor here because he isn't on track for tenure. He has already been removed from the school effective the end of this semester and won't be teaching again next year."

CHAPTER THIRTY

My brain is churning now. I've already had a weird feeling about Asher Vance and have been getting extremely suspicious of him, but this has only intensified it. I call Jackson with my suspicions, and he immediately confirms it was Warren Mason who lodged the complaint against Asher Vance when they were at the previous college.

"We were friends at the time, but I had no idea Asher Vance taught at that school. I didn't know the professor, and I didn't remember his name, but I knew about the complaint. Honestly, that was an extremely rough time in my life, a time I don't like looking back on, and my brain has done a lot of work to block out much of it. I wasn't particularly committed to school. I didn't take any of those classes, and I didn't really have a reason to know the professor's name, but the more I thought about it, the more familiar Vance seemed.

"That's what I had to go do. I needed to confirm that he was the one who Warren complained about all the time. He said he was a completely ridiculous teacher who had absurd expectations of his students. He didn't just try to challenge them, he tried to break them. And when they pushed back, he got aggressive and even violent. The reason Warren lodged the official complaint was Asher punched him after Warren stood up to him about a policy."

"Where are you now?" I ask.

"I'm trying to get in touch with his sister, Mallory. She was here when Callan was investigating."

"I remember reading about her in the notes," I say.

"I want to talk to her about what she remembers from that time. I might be able to get some details about exactly how that situation went down and what happened after. And then there's somewhere I need to be."

"You need to be careful, Jackson. You are being framed for these murders. He didn't say your name, but he outright accused you of being the one responsible for killing these people, and he seems to be inciting his students to be vigilantes. And now that this girl was attacked, I have a feeling things are going to get a lot worse," I say.

"I know. I'm fine, and I will be careful. I'll be back as soon as I can with more information," he says.

"You don't need to go searching for it, Jackson. I am in the FBI. I can get the information that we need. I have resources. And my cousin Dean is a private investigator and is the best in the business. He can find out anything," I tell him.

"I need to do this," he says.

He hangs up without giving me time to say anything else. I go back to the house and dig into Asher Vance's past. It isn't as easy as just a surface search, but I'm able to find online forums and even a few articles about the unsavory things that have happened in his past, including his assault on a student, who I now know was Warren Mason.

I sift back through the papers Callan found in Danielle's apartment and find a copy of a teacher's review that hadn't been submitted. It doesn't have his name, but it paints him very unkindly and provides enough context clues regarding what and how the unnamed man taught to tell me it's talking about Asher Vance. The review also heavily suggests she had reviewed him unfavorably before and didn't appreciate being forced to take his class again.

As I sit there going over each piece again, it all starts to fall into place. After checking himself out of the hospital, Asher Vance was planning for the year ahead even though he knew he isn't supposed to teach anymore. The school has already informed him that he is no longer a teacher there and would need to leave as soon as the semester is over, but he believes he can prove himself through teaching this case and be asked to stay on. He thinks he'll be able to publish about it and it will bring him the fame he is so hungry for. All the while, he would be able to get revenge on the people who have wronged him or done things he perceives as wrong.

I don't have enough concrete evidence to prove he is responsible. I'm working only on a theory, and I have to be extremely careful as I collect what I need to bring him down. Time is ticking, and I have a feeling something very big is about to happen.

I go back to the bloody passage I found in Asher Vance's office.

Now you are in my power, to slay or spare as I will! And I will kill you forthwith, unless you kneel and yield to me, confessing yourself to be a knight of little worth.
—Roger Lancelyn Green, *King Arthur and His Knights of the Round Table*

I try to get in touch with Jackson again, needing to know exactly what the falling out with the first victim was about. I know he doesn't want to talk about it, but that quote has me extremely concerned. The passage feels heavy-handed, like it is so dramatically declaring his intent to kill that it has to have another meaning. I go over it and over it, and suddenly something clicks.

When I was talking to Stephanie Campano, she mentioned a planning meeting today to prepare for the next year. The professors coming together just like the Knights of the Round Table.

"Shit," I mutter. "Now isn't the time to try to get involved, Jackson."

I keep trying to call him as I get to campus as fast as I can, but he still won't answer. I park on a road plastered with "No Parking" signs, not caring about the ticket I'll earn for blocking street cleaning. I run into the commons to the information desk and ask where the meeting is being held. I'm already backing away from the desk as the girl behind it starts to answer, and as soon as the full room number and building are out of her mouth, I turn and take off.

This is the grand finale—his intended capstone. He's going to kill the professors at the meeting because they all went against him. The message to Callan at the hospital was about more than just her. The gun was a reference to Jackson as well. I'm willing my phone to ring as I run to the building. His choice of Jackson to frame for the murders wasn't random and wasn't just about having a suspect to talk about. He has always intended to build up to this moment. I am praying with everything in me that I'm wrong, but my gut tells me he has lured Jackson into the meeting with one goal in mind.

If the person really responsible for the kills were dead, killed in self-defense by Asher's own hands, then he'd be a hero. He could tell everybody that he had known all along who was responsible and had put his own life on the line to protect everyone. That the authorities wouldn't listen to him and lives had been lost because he wasn't taken seriously. It would be so unfortunate that his fellow professors had to suffer and die, but at least he had survived and the culprit, the corrupt FBI agent with links to each of the victims, was dead.

The sound of gunshots and a scream tear through me almost the instant my boots hit the polished hallway floor. I call for emergency backup and then, my gun in my hand, sprint to the door and kick it open. Vance whips around to face me, and I plant my feet, holding my ground with the barrel of my gun pointed directly at his head.

"Put the gun down," I growl.

I notice blood pouring down from a wound in his shoulder. The placement makes it clearly a self-inflicted wound. It has stained the sleeve of his shirt fully red and drips onto the floor. At his feet lies Jackson. I don't let myself look at him further. Even a downward flicker of my eyes can be enough of a distraction for Asher to pull his trigger or advance on me.

"I'm so glad you're here, Emma," he says, my name sounding slick and grotesque coming out of his mouth. He sees us as equals.

"Put your weapon down *now*!"

"I had to protect myself. Don't you understand that?" he pleads. "I told you it was him. I knew it. He was betrayed by his best friend Warren in college. He was in love with Danielle, and she rejected him. He was envious of Dr. Brown for his wealth and success because it reminded him of his father. He thought that artist was scum and was bitter he didn't get punished for assaulting him all those years ago. He was so filled with rage that he just couldn't contain himself, and he was going to come here and kill everyone because we remind him of his failures. We remind him of what he could have been but what he will never be, because he threw it all away. He's an FBI agent, but that was never his dream."

"Shut up," I snap. "Put the gun down, or I will shoot it out of your hands."

"You would do that?" he asks. "When I risked my own life to save these people? My colleagues?"

"They aren't your colleagues. Not anymore. You got fired. Again. You weren't going to be teaching here anymore next year. You had been ousted from the academic community, and there was nobody else who was going to take you. Nobody cared about a single word that came out of your mouth anymore. You couldn't publish anything, and people were discrediting and making fun of you left and right. These people are what you could never be. And you hate them."

His eyes grow dark, the pleading look on his face melting into a vicious scowl. He lowers the gun to the table beside him and takes a step closer.

"Of course I hate them. The school was completely out of line, taking my position away from me. It's outrageous to bend to the whimpers of oversensitive, entitled students who believe they should be pampered and handed grades simply because they came into class. They should have been honored to be taught by me. Instead, they complained until the administration took away my opportunity at tenure, then not a single one of the faculty stood up for me. No one. I asked for their help. I asked for them to go to the administration and tell them the kind of man I actually am. How talented I am. How much of an asset I am to this school. And not a single one of them would do it," he says.

"Maybe because they didn't want to lie," I say.

"They did it because they are all envious. Not a single one of them is as intelligent as I am. None of them have the expertise I do. How many of them can say they have been recognized by a police department for making vital contributions to a murder investigation?" he asks. "Which of them could ever have done something like this? This is brilliance beyond comprehension.

"I created my own means of solidifying my legacy. My students could investigate a real case and show what an influential and powerful teacher I am. I even made sure there was a victim one of my students could rescue using the information I gave him in class. The case itself would go on to be studied for years to come. I would be the preeminent expert. It could define my entire future. I even crafted the perfect ending—a dead suspect with the final clue in his pocket. The only disappointment is, I couldn't share just how intricate it really is."

I'm disgusted by his avarice, by the gushing way he's describing himself, but it falls right in line with how he's been described.

"Stephanie," he continues, "she was always my first choice for whom to frame as the killer. Using the quotes, of course, came from her. She was exhausting to talk to. A passage or platitude for everything. As if those writers used up the English language centuries ago and now we have to recycle it for them rather than have our own thoughts. But that isn't why I wanted to see her suffer, of course. She spoke out against me. When I asked her to support me with the administration, she instead went behind my back and talked to the other faculty about ensuring I would be removed. She believed I was dangerous to the students," he says.

"No, she didn't," I say. "She never said anything like that to me. Should have no reason not to tell me that if that were true."

"That's what I heard," he says.

"You heard wrong. She might not have defended you, but she didn't speak to anybody about ousting you either. Where is she now?"

He points, and I glance over at the room long enough to see Stephanie's body sprawled on the carpet, unmoving, blood soaking the back of her dress.

"Now that she wasn't my suspect anymore, I decided to make her one of my victims. You see, I had no idea the kind of luck I really had. I started this, and then Jackson Blanchard walked back into my life. The man whose best friend ended the best part of my career and who stood by him while he did it, even after they stopped speaking. The man who I had just murdered.

"He was the perfect killer. What could be more dramatic than finding out the person responsible for all the murders was the one investigating them? It took some rearranging. Finding out he had interacted with Danielle was just an exquisite little gift from the universe. After that, I needed victims I could reasonably attribute to him."

"You killed just because they were connected to Jackson? Then why Danielle? Why the doctor?"

I have to keep him talking. As long as he's talking, he's not hurting anyone else and he's not trying to flee. If I can keep him talking, he will be here when the police arrive any minute. It doesn't matter if I get all the answers now. They'll all come out in the end.

"My reputation was tattered because I was too passionate about excellence. That was my crime. Expecting too much out of the people who plan to take over this world one day. And yet, Laurie Harrison could carry on an affair with a former student who was already in a long-term relationship and lying to everyone and had no consequences.

"The doctor knew about their relationship. He knew about her pregnancy. And yet he never said a single word about it. I found out because I was at the office on the day she came in for treatment. I told him he should expose them. Make it known. But he refused. He wouldn't hold them accountable for their actions. So I held him accountable for his."

Jackson groans on the ground, and I realize he's still alive. I bend down to check on him, and in that instant, Asher Vance snatches his own gun off the table. He takes a shot at me. I feel it graze my thigh, but he doesn't have a chance to take another shot. My bullet goes straight through his throat, and he drops dead where he stood.

I go over to Jackson and pull him into my lap. He has several gunshot wounds and is struggling to breathe. When I touch his jacket, I hear something crackle, and I pull out a torn piece of paper. I remember Vance's comment about the clue in his pocket and unfold it. Behind me I hear the police running down the hallway. I lean my head back against the cool classroom wall, close my eyes, and take a breath.

CHAPTER THIRTY-ONE

"'THERE WAS MUCH OF THE BEAUTIFUL, MUCH OF THE WANTON, much of the bizarre, something of the terrible, and not a little of that which might have excited disgust,' Edgar Allan Poe, *The Masque of the Red Death*."

When Jackson is out of the hospital, I will give him the paper I took out of his pocket and he can do with it what he wants. Until then, I have it in my safekeeping. Callan's eyes are round and filled with tears as I read the last of Vance's passages to her.

"You know," I say with a bitter laugh, "that was always my favorite of Poe's stories. It's going to hit a little differently when I read it now. But it is the perfect passage. Vance infected that group the way the character in the story infected the party in order to teach them a lesson. He wanted to ruin Stephanie Campano's life, but he ended up ending it."

"At least there were some survivors," Callan says. Three out of the seven teachers in that room did make it through the shooting. She drops her head back against the pillow, staring up at the ceiling. "They never should have been in that position. I should have stopped him."

"You can't think that way," I tell her.

"I was so close," she says. "I had gotten right there, but I couldn't make it. I was leaning toward Marcus. I thought he was trying to make himself more prominent and prime himself for a possible teaching job, but because I kept hearing that he loved to take over classes for Vance and he was known to act very much like him toward students. Then that paper I found in my bag. I knew he had to have put it in there."

"He didn't know what it was," I tell her. "I talked to him about it after everything happened before you woke up. He had found it on Vance's desk and wanted to ask him about it. He accidentally dropped it and ended up handing it to you when he helped you clean up. The clues were there. I was suspicious of him too."

"I really thought he was going to be down at that rally. I thought he had done something to Asher's disappearance and then was going after the politician. And when I didn't see him there, I thought I was wrong. I ended up preventing the politician from being murdered, but he still killed that man. I didn't even know who he was. He was just a random victim that he had to follow up with to keep the process going. Collateral damage."

"This was an incredibly difficult case. You were investigating someone who knew every step you were taking and could adjust what he was doing to stay ahead. His entire knowledge base is how to think like a killer who has gotten away with his crimes. You should be proud of what you accomplished," I say.

"I don't have anything to be proud of. You're the one who solved the case," she says.

"I took over for you. I didn't start from the beginning. If you hadn't done such exceptional work to start with, there would have been many more deaths."

She looks at me for a few seconds with her intense green eyes. Her short black hair makes them stand out even more. I see so much in those eyes. Regret. Sorrow. A deep pain she holds close. That's something I am very familiar with.

"I've spent my entire adult life looking up to you," she says.

"You have?" I ask.

"Yeah. I was on campus the day the bus station was bombed. I got so obsessed with that case. I had to find out what happened. And I found out about you. I followed everything you did in the Bureau, and you are such an inspiration. Knowing some of what you went through and seeing how you got yourself here… That was what I wanted to do, what I wanted to be. You are the reason I am an agent. I am beyond grateful you took over this case. I only wish I could have been better. I feel like I let you down," she says.

I give her a smile. "Listen to me. I have never been a perfect agent or person. I've done a lot of things I shouldn't have done, and I made mistakes in cases that I still cringe about. But I've had people beside me to hold me up and pull me through. I had the opportunity a while back to mentor a new agent. Aviva James. You would know her as Ava. I was horrible to her. I didn't see it at the time. I was angry. I was going through some of the most difficult times of my life, and I resented the idea of having this new, inexperienced woman tagging along behind me and getting in my way.

"I was mean to her. I was critical and unwelcoming. And that's being pretty kind to myself. That period of my life was like being the mean girl redemption B-story arc in a nineties teen movie—before the redemption. T. The thing is, I can look back on that now and see what I did to her. We're better now. She has her own team and is great at what she does. But I wish I had done better.

"And maybe you are that chance. Maybe now I can redeem myself. Because here's the thing, Callan. I might have inspired you, but you are where you are and who you are because of what's inside you. Agent Martinez didn't put you in charge of this case for any reason other than he believed in you. And he had every reason to. And still has every reason to. You are so different from me. You're just getting started. You're young, you're sharp. You take on a city that has broken many people before. You are exactly what the FBI needs. I believe you will be an amazing agent, and I will happily be here to watch it happen."

EPILOGUE

It's been two weeks since I left Richmond to come home to Sherwood. I have a feeling I'll be spending a lot more time in the city, and I'm looking forward to it. But for now, I'm knee-deep in helping Bellamy plan her long-awaited wedding to Eric. At this point, it feels like they've been engaged for as long as many people's first marriages, but it's finally about to happen.

I get home from a very long day of shopping in DC with Bellamy and Bebe to find a massive bag of food from the little Thai restaurant in town and a note from Sam on the kitchen table.

Ran away to my favorite place. Getting ready to have dinner with my favorite person.

I pick up the bag and carry it through the living room and up the steps toward my bedroom. Sam is already in his pajamas propped up on his side of the bed. I smile and lean in for a kiss.

"You couldn't even carry the food upstairs with you?" I ask.

"I thought it would be cuter this way," he says with a shrug.

I laugh. "Give me just a minute to get changed."

"All right. I'm going to put on the news. Do you mind?" he asks.

"No," I say, kicking off my shoes and starting to undress as I walk toward the bathroom for a quick shower. "Go ahead."

When I get out of the shower several minutes later and climb into bed next to Sam, I see he's watching a story about a missing woman.

"Sharon Bates was last seen at the Ultimate Bridal Expo convention four days ago. She was eagerly anticipating her upcoming wedding and attended the show alone. Friends and family say the twenty-five-year-old bride-to-be posted several times on social media from the show, making records of the vendors she was considering hiring. Her last post showed her picking up a boxed lunch from an attending caterer and saying she was going to take a quick break. She has not been heard from since."

"Maybe she just changed her mind," I say. "She could have thought it seemed like a good idea, but then she got into the convention with all that bridal stuff, and it just got to her."

"Maybe she's an overachiever and decided to be the world's most overeager runaway bride," Sam says. "Just go ahead and get that taken care of before going through all the effort of planning the wedding."

"She would definitely save money that way," I say.

"But if she did just run away," Sam says, the humor draining from his voice, "where is she?"

AUTHOR'S NOTE

Dear Reader,

Thank you for choosing to read *The Girl and the Secret Passage,* the fourth installment in this new season of the Emma Griffin® FBI Mystery series. This time around, I decided to mix things up a bit. We had several chapters taking place in the past from a perspective other than Emma's interwoven into the overarching storyline. I intended it to help capture the complexity of the investigation. But it's a departure from my usual writing style, and I would love to hear your thoughts on this approach.

I owe Emma and the rest of this beloved cast of characters to your unyielding support and enthusiasm. So, if you could please take a quick moment to leave a review for this book, I would appreciate it enormously. Your reviews allow me to keep living my dream as an indie author and bringing you the thrilling mystery stories that you love.

While you eagerly await the next Emma Griffin book, I invite you to catch up with Emma's cousin in the *Dean Steele Mystery Thriller series!* The latest book, titled *The Killer Among Us,* is slated to release in December and will be a whodunnit mystery that you won't want to miss. Dean finds himself at a Christmas party unlike any other. With a snowstorm approaching and guests mysteriously vanishing as the night deepens, our favorite PI is caught right in the middle of it. It's a thrilling situation with a rising body count, and Dean's got to navigate it all while the storm rages on. Sound intriguing? I thought so!

I promise to keep bringing you heart-pounding, mind-bending mysteries that will keep you at the edge of your seat, and coming back for more!

Yours,
A.J. Rivers

P.S. If for some reason you didn't like this book or found typos or other errors, please let me know personally. I do my best to read and respond to every email at mailto:aj@riversthrillers.com

P.P.S. If you would like to stay up-to-date with me and my latest releases I invite you to visit my Linktree page at *www.linktr.ee/a.j.rivers* to subscribe to my newsletter and receive a free copy of my book, Edge of the Woods. You can also follow me on my social media accounts for behind-the-scenes glimpses and sneak peeks of my upcoming projects, or even sign up for text notifications. I can't wait to connect with you!

ALSO BY
A.J. RIVERS

Emma Griffin FBI Mysteries

Season One

Book One—The Girl in Cabin 13*
Book Two—The Girl Who Vanished*
Book Three—The Girl in the Manor*
Book Four—The Girl Next Door*
Book Five—The Girl and the Deadly Express*
Book Six—The Girl and the Hunt*
Book Seven—The Girl and the Deadly End*

Season Two

Book Eight—The Girl in Dangerous Waters*
Book Nine—The Girl and Secret Society*
Book Ten—The Girl and the Field of Bones*
Book Eleven—The Girl and the Black Christmas*
Book Twelve—The Girl and the Cursed Lake*
Book Thirteen—The Girl and The Unlucky 13*
Book Fourteen—The Girl and the Dragon's Island*

Season Three

Book Fifteen—The Girl in the Woods*
Book Sixteen —The Girl and the Midnight Murder*
Book Seventeen— The Girl and the Silent Night*
Book Eighteen — The Girl and the Last Sleepover*
Book Nineteen — The Girl and the 7 Deadly Sins*
Book Twenty — The Girl in Apartment 9*
Book Twenty-One — The Girl and the Twisted End*

Emma Griffin FBI Mysteries Retro - Limited Series
(Read as standalone or before Emma Griffin book 22)

Book One— *The Girl in the Mist**
Book Two— *The Girl on Hallow's Eve**
Book Three— *The Girl and the Christmas Past**
Book Four— *The Girl and the Winter Bones**
Book Five— *The Girl on the Retreat**

Season Four

Book Twenty-Two — *The Girl and the Deadly Secrets**
Book Twenty-Three — *The Girl on the Road**
Book Twenty-Four — *The Girl and the Unexpected Gifts*
Book Twenty-Five — <u>*The Girl and the Secret Passage*</u>

Ava James FBI Mysteries

Book One—*The Woman at the Masked Gala**
Book Two—*Ava James and the Forgotten Bones**
Book Three —*The Couple Next Door**
Book Four — *The Cabin on Willow Lake**
Book Five — *The Lake House**
Book Six — *The Ghost of Christmas**
Book Seven — *The Rescue**
Book Eight — *Murder in the Moonlight**
Book Nine — *Behind the Mask**

Dean Steele FBI Mysteries

Book One—*The Woman in the Woods**
Book Two — *The Last Survivors*
Book Three — *No Escape*
Book Four — *The Garden of Secrets*

ALSO BY
A.J. RIVERS & THOMAS YORK

Bella Walker FBI Mystery Series

Book One—The Girl in Paradise*
Book Two—Murder on the Sea*

Other Standalone Novels
Gone Woman
* Also available in audio

Made in the USA
Monee, IL
19 November 2023